S0-BXT-651

Few Things Left Unsaid

was your promise of love fulfilled?

Also by Sudeep Nagarkar

That's the Way We Met

Few Things Left Unsaid

was your promise of love fulfilled?

SUDEEP NAGARKAR

RANDOM HOUSE INDIA

Published by Random House India in 2013
Ninth impression in 2015
First published by Srishti Publishers & Distributors,
New Delhi, in 2011

Copyright © Sudeep Nagarkar 2011

Random House Publishers India Pvt. Ltd.
7th Floor, Infinity Tower C
DLF Cyber City
Gurgaon 122 002, Haryana, India

Random House Group Limited
20 Vauxhall Bridge Road
London SW1V 2SA
United Kingdom

978 81 8400 419 9

This book is sold subject to the condition that it shall not, by way of
trade or otherwise, be lent, resold, hired out, or otherwise circulated
without the publisher's prior consent in any form of binding or cover
other than that in which it is published and without a similar condition
including this condition being imposed on the subsequent purchaser.

Typeset in Adobe Garamond Pro by SwaRadha Typesetting, New Delhi

Printed and bound in India by Replika Press Private Limited

A PENGUIN RANDOM HOUSE COMPANY

To the girl I'm still in search of...

Tujhko pahne ke liye, khudko kho chukka hu,
Yakeen kar tujhe apna banakar tujhme khona chahta hoon.
Saal guzar gaye tere aankhon me aankhein daale,
Bas ek baar nazar se nazar milaana chaahta hoon.

Contents

And I Can't Stop Loving You

Why do I love you? Why do I want you?
You've always lived in my heart,
Then why did I let you go?

Why do I still care for you?
Why do I still wait for you?
Why do I still think of you?
When I know, you will never come back.

Maybe you weren't mine.
My life is just wasted and it's all true,
Wondering why I exist?
Why does my heart beat?
When I had lost my sweetheart,
Who was more important than this bloody heart.

Why I am ready to die for you?
Why I am ready to fly for you?

When I know I can't do that.
Still I wish I had done something for you.

Why do I love you? Why do I want you?
You've always lived in my heart.
Then why did I let you go?

Now, being single, I think,
Why did I let you go?

In Remembrance

'Why are you so stubborn? Don't you understand you are heading towards a dead end?' shouted Sameer. I was not in my senses and everything around me was in a haze. My mouth was reeking of alcohol. We were sitting on a small bench besides a garage where we usually hung out in the evening. It was like our own personal smoking lounge.

Sameer, my friend from the past six years, was an average looking person with an okay dressing sense, spectacles, cropped hair, and a weird English accent that I would always make fun of. I liked him because he was sincere and honest. As the proverb goes, 'A friend in need is a friend indeed'.

But at the present moment, things were turning sour between us. He raised his voice and said, 'If you just want to do what you feel like and not listen to what I have to say, then get lost. I am leaving.'

'Okay sorry,' I replied. 'I understand it's not right, but I just don't have the strength to face the real world. Not anymore.'

He gave me some water and the argument continued.

If I think about it practically, I was really taking my life to that end of the road from which there was no turning back.

I kept telling myself: No, I don't love her. I don't want her back. I am happy and enjoying my life. Who says my heart is broken? To hell with her! I will sleep with other girls. And why should I think of just one girl when she doesn't give a damn about me as well?

But the fact was that I was just fooling myself by saying all this. I have always loved and cared for her, and I always will. Why do we love a person so much? I had no answer to that. I still wonder why did I let her go.

When I had called her on Spetember 10 to convince her to come back to my life and rescue me from the darkness, she had said, 'You never loved me. It was just lust. You loved my outer appearance, not who I was on the inside. You hurt me, my feelings, and my love for you. You would not have ignored me otherwise.'

I had replied furiously saying, 'No bachcha, I never tried to ignore you. But if you still think I did, I am ready to do whatever you want me to. You really think I loved you for your looks? I won't justify myself but you know what the truth is.'

'What matters is trust. And that you broke so easily. Trust, relationships, and the heart are three things that one should respect. But you broke all three and left me alone. Now just buzz off,' she had shouted.

'Fine, I won't ever disturb you again. But before leaving, just tell me one thing—do you seriously not love me any more?' I had asked. In my heart, I had really wanted her to say 'Yes, I miss you, I want you, and I am all yours.'

But she had unfortunately said, 'No, I don't. I do not even care for you now. Please leave me alone. Bye.'

I remember thinking to myself: What the fuck is this! Lust... love...what does she mean? I love her. Never did I once lust for her. Did she mean that whatever she felt for me was lust? Maybe I don't deserve to be her boyfriend. She loved me. She really did. I hope she did. But she says she did not. How is that possible? Is it the end of everything? Is it the end of happiness? End of our friendship? End of our relationship? Maybe it is the end of life for me...

That was the time I decided to take some firm decisions in my life.

As the Supreme Court verdict goes, 'Dafa 302, sazaa-e-maut—to be hanged till death...'

To you it may seem silly, like I have gone crazy. But it sounded like the verdict from my broken heart.

'SAZAA-E-MAUT. DRINK TILL DEATH.'

For life goes on...

I fell on the floor with a bang. My last words were, 'I love you, I really love you. I never betrayed you. The situation was against me. Trust me, my bachcha, I am still crazy about you. My heart still skips a beat whenever I see you.'

But nobody was there to hear me. Nobody took me seriously. And I cried my heart out...

Raat itni tanhaa kyun hoti hai?
Kismat se apni sabko shikaayat kyun hoti hai?
Ajeeb khel khelti hai kismat!
Jise hum paa nahi sakte,
Usi se mohabbat kyun hoti hai?

So Close, Yet So Far

October 11—a day which held the utmost importance in my life. I had been waiting for it since what seemed like forever and had done all the preparations for it. After all, it was Riya's birthday. As I was five months younger to her in age, she used to tease me a lot about it. 'You are younger, follow my orders', she'd say. Three days prior to her birthday, I got thinking about what gift to buy for her. I searched a lot, and finally got a little teddy bear for 500 rupees from an Archies gift gallery. I even made her a handmade greeting card which said:

Forgive me for all the things I did.
I'm sorry for all the pain I caused you.
No sooner than you went away,
I realized your importance in my life.
Please give me my life back.

I need it. I miss it. And I miss you.

Yours,
Aditya

෨

I woke up early in the morning. In anticipation of her birthday, I was unable to catch much sleep. I was anxious, afraid, excited, happy, nervous—all at the same time.

I plugged my cellphone earphones in my ears and drove my bike to Navi Mumbai where her house was located. I was continuously listening to our favourite song—*Tujhe dekh dekh sona, tujhe dekh kar hai jagna, Maine ye zindagani sang tere bitaani, tujhme basi hai meri jaan...*

Then I looked at my watch. It was 2.30 pm. Nervously smoking a cigarette, I dismounted from my bike and came and stood right in front of her apartment.

A cigarette later, I saw the time on my watch. It was 2.40 pm.

Ten cigarettes later, I saw the time again. It was 3.30 pm.

One cold drink and fifteen cigarettes later, 4.10 pm.

Two cold drinks and twenty cigarettes later, 4.40 pm.

I thought of giving up. Sameer, who had been waiting with me for over two hours, motivated me to continue.

'She will come, dude. Just have patience.'

'Why is it always me? Why can't I get to talk to my love on her birthday?'

But I knew it was my mistake. It was all because I had taken the worst decision of my life. I was the one who had left her all alone. Why should I blame anyone else?

By the time it was 4.50 pm, I took my mobile and dialled her number.

'Is it ringing?' Sameer asked.

'Not yet.'

'Is it now?' Sameer whispered after a few seconds.

'Ssshhh…wait, its ringing.'

I could hear her hello tune.

Jab rulaana hi tha tujhe, to phir hasaaya kyun, saath rehkar bhi hai juda, to pass aaya kyun…

My heartbeats increased. I heard a sound at the other end. 'Hello?' I said in anticipation, but all I got was an automated response saying, 'The number you have dialled is currently busy'.

What the fuck! I will throw my cell away. Why me, why always me?

'Aditya, she's here! Run,' shouted Sameer when he saw her coming out from her apartment.

Yes, she was there. Dressed in a white top, low waist jeans, black bag, wearing black eyeliner, and her hair left loose. She was looking hot enough to drive me crazy. I was confused about how I should react. So I just ran away from there. It was a straight road with a curve at the end that led towards other apartments.

We stopped near the curve and watched her come towards us. My heartbeats turned faster. She came closer to me and I felt like I missed a heartbeat and would die right there.

I was paralysed. I didn't know what to do. She was getting into an autorickshaw.

Damn, all in vain! I thought.

I gathered courage and ran in her direction with a box of chocolates in one hand and a wrapped gift in the other.

'Riya, please wait,' I shouted after her.

'Bhaiya, HDFC bank chaloge?' she said to the driver.

'Please wait. Just give me two minutes. Please,' I cried.

'I am late, Aditya. Please, I can't do this now.'

'I just want two minutes of your time. I promise.'

'Okay fine. Get into the rickshaw. You can come with me till HDFC.'

I got in. The bank was hardly one kilometre away. But it was still better than not getting a chance to speak to her at all.

'How are you?' I inquired.

'Enjoying my life.'

I knew what it meant. She just wanted to show that she did not care for me anymore. She just wanted me to stop bothering her.

'Oh really? So whats the plan for today?' I asked her, wanting to hear her say, 'Nothing, spending the day with my friends. You're free to join us.' But she responded with, 'I don't want to tell you. So don't bother asking.'

This was the worst answer anyone could expect. Seriously. However, I was helpless. If I would have overreacted at that time, she would have thrown me out of the auto that minute itself. I had waited for this moment for a long time and I knew better than to ruin it. Therefore, I chose to remain mum. But the heart is a fool.

I shouted, 'Why are you so rude?'

'Aditya, it's my birthday and I am going out with my friends. So please don't spoil my day.'

Was I spoiling her day? I thought I would make her day special by giving her a surprise. But you can never really understand girls, can you? They are divine creations of God—mysterious and incomprehensible.

'Happy birthday!' I wished her.

'Thanks. Now get down. We've reached HDFC.'

She told the rickshaw driver to wait and went to the ATM. I was still waiting for her by the auto. When she came out, I could tell that she was bit annoyed watching me still waiting there.

'You haven't left? Just leave, please. Don't make me more angry than I already am.'

'These are for you,' I said handing her the gifts I had brought for her. I was keeping my fingers crossed since I was not sure whether she would accept them or not.

'Thanks, but I can't take them.'

I knew she would say that but I kept on insisting, 'Please take them, please.'

'No, I can't. I will take these chocolates but not this big wrapped thing. Sorry.'

'Riya, I bought these especially for you.'

'So what? Throw it away.' My heart cried in pain. I was helpless. I needed her. I needed her even more badly than before. My heart needed her the most.

She went away. I kept thinking if I should be happy that I saw her or sad that it turned out to be a bad surprise for her. Or should I think of all the money I wasted in buying her those gifts that she didn't even bother taking? I could have made good use of the money and purchased four bottles of beer instead.

Why God? Why me? I cried to myself.

I will drink till I'm dead, I thought.

But was it really the end of life?

Nothing is permanent. Maybe my love story will take a new turn and I will have a happy ending after all. Or will it be vice versa? I was really trapped. My life had come to a standstill.

How should I get Riya back into my life? I thought about it a bit more.

But why did I let her go?

I always dreamt of falling in love and when I was in love, everything felt like a dream. It was a dream world with no limits. I got a girl who deserved a better person than me. Still she chose to be with me. I was her life. What happened then? Why did I do this to her? The dream ended in a way I never wanted it to. Nevertheless, the dream hurt for it was not real. So does falling in love hurt? After all, it is a fall. I now realized why people call it 'falling in love'. I got my answers when I was left hurt and crushed from the inside, bleeding all alone…

A Surprise Encounter

I was just about to sit and study for my fourth semester paper when I got an SMS from Riya.

```
I always loved you, will always do. However,
I will never come back. In fact, I cannot come
back in your life ever again. Please move ahead
without me. AND PLEASE STOP DRINKING AND SMOKING
SO MUCH.
```

I closed the book in my lap and started to think of who had told Riya that I drank or smoke too much. But I could not guess who.

Finally the exam day came. I had studied almost three chapters that usually carried a weightage of 40 marks. I knew I was going to screw up the paper badly. But fortune favours the brave. The three chapters that I had studied accounted for almost 80 marks in the paper. Now I was sure of clearing the subject and getting the golden figure of 40.

It was time to have a blast on the big new years' night leaving all negativity behind me.

My friends and I spent the night as if it was the last day of our life. Food, chicken, beer, cigarettes—everything was devoured with hunger. I was driving my bike back home from the party at around 3 am. I stopped on the highway to smoke. I was just resting on my bike and was not really in my senses from all that drinking. A stranger tapped my shoulder from behind. I turned around to see a well-built man in his mid 40s wearing a white shirt, black trousers, and Woodland shoes.

He was looking into my eyes deeply. I could tell he was drunk too. Finally, he broke the silence.

'What is your problem, son?'

I was confused and said nothing.

'Are you in love?' he questioned me.

How does he know I'm in love? I've never met him. I've never seen him before.

'Tell me son, I can see you are not happy,' he continued.

What exactly is happening? I was a bit shocked. If he turned out to be dad's friend spying on me, then I knew I was going to get flushed out of my house.

'I am deeply in love,' I answered back.

'Then what's the problem? She does not love you or what? Or you never told her you loved her? Why are you becoming a devdas?'

This was too much for me to take. I really did not have an answer to all those questions. Who is this man? Was I really looking like devdas? What the fuck is happening!

'Nothing uncle. She loves me too. However, she cannot come back to me and I can't bear this pain anymore. I am just living for my parents now.'

'You have to. They are the ones who care for you. They are the ones who live for you. They are the ones who work hard for your future. They are the ones who will have many expectations from you. They are the ones who gave you your life.'

Tears rolled down my eyes. I knew whatever he said was true. I realized I could not ignore all that he had said right now.

'I am a 48-year-old Bengali, and we are born romantics.'

Does he mean a 'born' devdas? Not again, I thought. Two devdas' standing in middle of the road at 3 am discussing Paro. Thank God late night Chandramukhis were not in the scene.

'I loved a girl once, maybe a hundred times more than you do. But today I cannot go back to her, even if she calls me back. I have my family. I cannot leave them. My son. My wife. I just can't leave them alone and go after her.'

'True,' I said.

'Look my son, love is never wrong. But a girl can be. Remember these words all your life.'

What did he say just now? Did I even hear what he said?

Love is never wrong but a girl can be.

These words went straight into my heart.

'Just carry on with your life. Don't give up. You still have a long life ahead of you.'

Now I turned serious. Is he a human or an angel from heaven who has descended on earth to show me the right path? Who is he?

I did not know him, had never seen him before in my life. Why was he showing me what lay ahead when I never believed in God in the first place? Though Riya trusted Lord Ganesha a lot, I didn't. Then why did this person from nowhere suddenly land up in front of me? Was it to reaffim my faith in God?

'If I were in your shoes, I would have dated some model lookalike since you're quite handsome yourself. So why are you ruining your life? Move ahead my son, move ahead,' the man said fishing out something from his pocket. 'Here, this is my card. Keep it with you. I will be happy if you call me tomorrow.'

And then he left. I was still standing there watching him fade into the darkness. Bringing my life closer to me. A lot closer than I would have expected. Then I laid flat on my bike and closed my eyes just to comprehend what had really happened a few minutes back.

Is she wrong or me? Riya can't be wrong. She is too sweet to be wrong. She did everything for me. I never did anything for her. I wished I had though. I just gave her pain and nothing else. How can such a sweet girl like her be wrong? I will never believe it. Never have and never will. I was wrong. It was me.

I took his card out from my pocket. It said:
Mr Banerjee, Sales Manager.

I reached home thinking about our situation. That night, I could not sleep. I just wanted to relive whatever I had gone through. From the very beginning.

I sat on my sofa, closed my eyes, and went back to the days after my class 12 board exams when I was struggling to get admission to a decent college somewhere.

Rat Race

I had heard from friends that degree colleges were like a girl's skirt. Men just want to see what is under it. Is the view nice? Is the service good? The rat race of getting into a good college almost reaches a point of obsession at times. Moreover, once you are obsessed, it is difficult to get it out of your mind. However, after seeing the same skirt for almost four years, you tend to get bored and ultimately just want to get out of it.

I had also heard that in engineering, 80 percent of the final exam was based on the one lecture you missed and the one book you did not read.

I had also read somewhere a few funny things about engineering. A group of managers were given an assignment to measure the height of a flagpole. They attacked the challenge with ladders and tape measures. Soon they were falling off the ladders, dropping the tape measures—the whole thing was just a mess.

An engineer came along and saw what they were trying to do, walked over, pulled the flagpole out of the ground, laid it flat, measured it from end to end, gave the measurement to one of the managers and walked away.

After the engineer had gone, one manager turned to another and laughed. 'Isn't that just like an engineer? We're looking for the height and he gives us the length.'

But my parents were adamant I do engineering. I was just waiting for the first list to be displayed in colleges, I was praying hard to see my name on the list for I had studied hard for the high school exams and had achieved good scores to get through an engineering college of my choice.

The day finally arrived. I browsed the website to check the list and see what the future had in store for me. However, the server was very slow and I was unable to view the page. I waited for a few minutes and the site finally asked me to enter my application number.

I was scared because I didn't know whether would I be placed in a good college in Mumbai or somewhere else. I did not really want to leave my parents and stay away from home. I clicked on the tab to get the 'results' option. It was the scariest moment of my life uptil then. I was looking at the screen of my computer. My mom was looking at me. Her look made me more nervous. My dad was out of town. I really wanted him close to me for support.

When the result finally came up, I stared in shock at the computer screen.

Not placed in any college.

How could this be? I looked at my mom and saw tears in her eyes. She retraced her steps to her bedroom. Never in my wildest dreams did I think this would be the result. I had scored good marks in the exams. I thought that maybe it wasn't the fault of the colleges. Maybe I had filled up the form wrong. I really had a good score to get through some college—if not in Mumbai then atleast somewhere outside Mumbai. I was scared to face my mom. Still I went to her with courage, and on seeing that she was crying, I consoled her. The second list was still to be displayed. Maybe I would be lucky in that one.

I called Sameer to inquire about his result.

'Hey Sameer, did u get placed?'

'I was about to call you. I got placed in Euro College, Navi Mumbai. What about you?' he said.

Hearing this, I just ended the call. The realization that he had secured admission and I hadn't disturbed me. It was not fair, especially since he had scored less than me. Still he had got through. And I had not. This made me extremely jealous.

He is an OBC, so maybe he got through the quota.

Sameer had taken all his friends, including me, to celebrate of his placement in a good college. Even though I was in no mood to party, I reluctantly agreed since Sameer was a good friend. We had fun the whole night. Sameer asked me to booze. But I did not. Firstly, I really hated boozing. I thought it was a waste of money and time. Secondly, I was still disturbed about the results that had come in the morning. Not just me, I knew my entire family was disturbed.

'Don't worry yaar, you will get through a good college. Just relax and enjoy the moment,' assured Sameer.

It's very easy to say things like these, especially when you're not on the receiving end, but difficult to put into practice. I tried to enjoy myself at the party and mixed with everyone around. But somewhere at the back of my mind, I was aware that I had not lived up to the expectations of my parents. I did not want to take admission through the management quota where about two to three lakh rupees donation was asked.

The next morning, my mom gave me a letter that had arrived by courier. I opened it and saw my Business of Management test results. Even though I had applied to various engineering colleges, I had also given the BMS entrance exam. I had been offered admission into three colleges out of which two were among the top five. I was excited to tell my mom about this. But when she saw the letter, she gave me a very cold shrug, like she was not interested in it.

My parents had never supported me in my decision of doing anything except engineering. I somehow tried to convince my parents by telling them the benefits of BMS and showing them why it was better than engineering. However, they were firm in their decision. 'My son will be an engineer,' said dad who was an engineer himself and wanted to see his son take up the same profession. But I never understood what engineering was. I tried to convince them a lot but all in vain. 'NO BMS. AND THAT'S FINAL,' asserted dad.

Soon it was the day when the second admission list of engineering colleges was going to be displayed. Once again, I was in front of my computer. I really wanted to get through this time. I clicked on the 'result' option on the screen.

EURO COLLEGE

I saw a glimpse of happiness in my mom's eyes. She screamed in joy, 'Finally my son will be an engineer.' Even though it was something I never really wanted, I was happy to see my mom so happy. I was going to be an engineer after all!

For an optimist the glass is half full, for a pessimist it's half empty. And for an engineer it is twice bigger than necessary.

I made up my mind that I would work hard to be an engineer. One big plus point was that girls are attracted to engineers. Maybe it was because it was an honourable post to have. But surely some girls thought otherwise since an engineer works from 6.30 am to 7.30 pm daily, leaving one with no time for morning kisses, evening walks, and cuddling at night with one's partner.

Even before I had officially joined college, I wished for some good looking girls with nice curves in my class. Thus, being in the Electronics department increased my chances of being near them. As expected, there were more girls in the Electronics branch than in other fields like Mechanical and Civil. Computer and IT had almost same intake of girls as in Electronics. However, those in IT and Computer were said to have nice curves and a fairer skin than Electonics. Sameer opted for Civil Engineering. He planned to do Civil Engineering ever since he knew what he wanted to do in life. I never wanted engineering itself.

But I was satisfied with my destiny for three reasons. First, I saw my parents happy. Second, I had got into the same college where Sameer was. Third, I got a branch where girls would be in plenty. Having to spend four years without girls would have made life very difficult. To live without seeing curves, skirts, and cleavage was impossible for me.

College was going to start from August 3. I wanted to make a good impression on girls from the first day. I purchased new shirts, T-shirts, denims, and Woodland shoes. All this preparation was to make a good impact on the girls. I wanted my first impression to be the best.

The first day arrived. I was expected to reach college by 10.30 am, so accordingly, I left my house at 9.30 am.

It was raining heavily. On my way to college, I thought about how my parents' dream had come true. It was their dream that I study in an engineering college. The first lecture was supposed to be conducted at 11 am. I was there by 10.15 am. I entered the class excitedly.

The college campus was not as good as I had expected. The entrance to the building was tricky. There were too many gates. I was confused from where to enter and exit. The seniors informed us that we had to assemble in the quadrangle. A list of names containing divisions that were allotted to everyone was displayed. There was a huge crowd gathered near the quadrangle. I preferred to stay away from it. I was just glancing at girls closely. Girls of all shapes and sizes. Girls wearing tight jeans. Girls with cute smiles. They all seemed excited, like they were envisioning themselves as future engineers. Everyone was busy in his or her own world. Then a group of seniors arrived.

They told a few of us to join them on the second floor. Classrooms on that floor were numbered S1, S2, S3 and so on. Similarly there were F1, F2, F3 numbered classes on the first floor. We entered S3. We were almost 15 students, which included one girl. I finally understood why we had been called to the classroom. RAGGING.

One of the seniors came towards me. He was well built, almost 6 feet tall, and had long hair that fell till his shoulders. I was asked to stand separately in the left corner of the classroom. One girl was also asked to do the same. She was wearing a red tank top and low waist jeans. She had perfect curves and a nice butt. But I was confused about what was happeneing. Why have we been made to stand separately? The rest of the students were asked to strip. A sense of relief went through me thinking I had been saved from the suffering.

If I had to strip, it would have been embarrassing because I was wearing green-coloured underwear. I would have been the centre of attraction. Nevertheless, I was safe now. I was still worried as to what they would ask me to do if not strip. I hoped it wouldn't be anything worse than that. The students were forced to stand outside the classroom facing the quadrangle so that all the freshers standing in the quadrangle were able to watch the scene. It was the scariest moment for me as I anticipated public humiliation. I glanced at the girl standing on the opposite corner and asked her name and place of residence. She told me that her name was Nikita and was from Mulund in Central Mumbai. Mulund was almost 8 kilometres away from college and 5 kilometres from my house. She looked as afraid as a person in a lion's den. I could see fear in her eyes. It was equally tough for me to face that situation.

Gradually, all the students left the classroom. Nikita and I were the only ones left with the seniors. I was told to propose to the girl standing beside me. Nikita was afraid as she was told to kiss me after I proposed. But

I was excited. The first day in college and you get a kiss from one of the hottest bombshells. What more could a guy ask for? But to my dismay, she was also told to slap me hard after I kissed her back. I was tense. I hadn't anticipated getting a slap from her.

Plus it would reduce my chances of getting closer to her in the future. However, I had to face it. I was planning to give her the best kiss of her life. Maybe a slight peck on the cheek or a deep passionate kiss on the lips.

I went closer to her and said, *I LOVE YOU*.

The seniors were not satisfied with my performance. They wanted something different.

And so I tried something different. I said, 'I want to spend my entire life with you. Will you allow me to do so?'

This was also rejected. Then I remembered something special.

'I want to ask you one question. Can I?' I asked Nikita.

She replied in the affirmative saying, 'Yes you can.'

'Okay listen then, once there were two birds in a house. One was called 'I LOVE YOU' and the other 'YOU LOVE ME'. Then 'YOU LOVE ME' flew away. So tell me who is left in the house?

I thought I had made a big mistake. I just looked at the seniors. They were looking at me. In fact 'staring' at me. And suddenly everyone started laughing. I calmed down. I was waiting for Nikita to answer.

'I LOVE YOU.'

The seniors shouted, 'C'mon kiss him. Don't waste time.'

She came and stood close to me. Every girl grows up thinking of her first kiss being magical.

Was this her first kiss? I did not dare ask her. She came closer. I could see fear in her eyes. Maybe it was her first kiss after all.

I whispered in her ears in the calmest voice I could manage, 'Don't worry about it. It's not a big deal, let's just do it and get over with it. I'll be nice, I promise'. She felt a bit comfortable hearing this. We both were thinking who would kiss first. Finally, being a guy, I took the initiative and locked my lips with hers. She closed her eyes. I grabbed her shoulders and let her lips touch mine, softly, gently. Then I jammed my tongue down her throat. And the teeth... Oh God, the teeth. It was as if I had run full force, mouth-open into a gorge. I felt her respond by her rolling tongue inside my mouth. I could tell it was not her first kiss for sure. Moreover, this was not my first kiss either. I returned her response with a deep passionate kiss. All of it felt like a dream scenario.

'Stop it. We've seen enough!' I heard someone shout. I wanted this kiss to continue.

However, I had to stop. She opened her eyes. She was blushing. I knew she had liked it. There was a spark in her eyes. Had she fallen in love with me or was it the after-effect of the kiss? She was looking deep into my eyes. There was a deep silence in the classroom. A moment later, she slapped me across my right cheek. It was such a hard slap that I almost lost my balance and fell down. I was shocked. But I had to face it. It was a tight slap. We were asked to leave. And we both did. I tried to follow Nikita but she went away without caring to stop.

Am I a bad kisser? She did not even bother to look back once. Am I in love? Maybe I simply wanted her to go to bed with me. She was an excellent kisser.

I went down to the quadrangle and noted down the subjects and the timetable. My classes were to start from 11 am and end by 6 pm. Studying for 7 hours was a difficult task. In addition to that, the names of all the five subjects seemed like complicated names of medicines to me. I hated all of them.

1. APPLIED MATHEMATICS 1
2. APPLIED SCIENCE 1
3. BEE
4. CP1
5. APPLIED MECHANICS

My section was E. Roll no. 36.

As it was the first day of college, classes started at around 2 pm after which there was a short lunch break.

The classroom resembled a movie hall with each row more elevated than the one below it. I went and took a seat in the last row from where each student in the classroom could be seen clearly. I was especially looking at all the girls. I was happy to see that there were a few nice looking girls in my class. Sameer was in a different section than mine. I started talking to a guy sitting besides me. He told me his name was Swapnil. He was average looking. Almost of same height as me—5 feet 6 inches. He seemed very friendly. He also stayed near my place—central Mumbai.

The first lecture was quite boring. I paid a deaf ear to what the professor was saying. He was teaching something related to BJT transistors. He had drawn some funny looking block diagrams on the board and was telling us the advantages of BJT and how it works. I hated everything. I wondered how I was going to spend 4 years in that college. After the lecture was over, there were BEE practicals from 4 pm to 6 pm.

When I saw the lab, all my admiration for the college was gone. Forget about chairs, the lab didn't even have fans, at least none that worked anyway. Seriously speaking, it was very tough to convince myself that I was going to spend my days in that place. I had never imagined a college like this. One positive thing was that I had talked to some of my seniors and they were all very optimistic about their prospects after graduating from this college and that I would slowly but surely enjoy my days here. They believed that the college's biggest advantage was that it had a great alumni base.

I had befriended a couple of other guys in my class— Swapnil and Anup—and the number of friends in my group had increased to three. Not bad, I thought, as they were good friends. I had a good time with them on the first day. With Sameer, we formed a group of four.

Attending lectures regularly from 10.30 am to 6 pm was like watching the same movie in a multiplex everyday. Bunking classes became a regular habit. I never understood what made those first benchers sit for lectures. There was nothing interesting that was being said.

It was Monday morning, time for the first lecture of the day. Swapnil was dozing as usual. And so was I. Swapnil was thinking of ways to bunk the lecture. I thought he was out of his mind!. The first benchers would never cooperate with him. They were paying such rapt attention to the professor during the lecture that it almost felt like they were watching Shakira move her hips in front of them.

I wanted to know what was running through Swapnil's mind. He was very smart at these things. After the first lecture, we had practicals. As we reached the practicals room, he told me to send an SMS to one student from each batch. It said:

Mass bunk after the break. Forward the message to your entire class.

A few students were afraid of mass bunking. They feared their attendance would go down and they would get less marks in the term paper. These were the most irritating students in the class. Every engineering college has a few students like them. I never understood what they got by buzzing around the professors like a bee all the time. For a few extra marks, they were willing to do anything it seemed. Swapnil warned them not to sit for the lectures. Still I thought they would ignore his message. They had done it once before too. We had spread the word for a mass bunk and six students had sat for the lecture without paying heed to the message. This time we were serious. We convinced everyone from our batch.

The practicals were over. Our entire class was standing outside our classroom and we told all of them not to attend the next lectures. Looking at the majority standing outside, those 'six' nerdy and troublesome students were not able to enter the class. So they went back home. We were still standing in front of the door and did not want a single student to sit in class. Ten minutes were left for the lecture to begin. We told everyone to vacate the corridor. Almost 10 of us went to the second floor to check if the professor was going back to the staff room.

When the professor came, he saw that the classroom was locked. He opened it, only to find the classroom empty. He was still standing there to see if any one was around. Almost 10 minutes later, he saw a student. He gestured for the boy to come to him. From behind the pillar, where all of us had been hiding and watching the proceedings, we saw the professor and the student talking about something. But we were too far to hear what was being said.

After the professor left, we rushed to the student and asked him what the professor was saying.

'He has asked me to tell everyone that tomorrow we all have to submit an assignment as punishment.'

'A punishment assignment?' Swapnil asked.

'Yes, we have to solve 5 problems from the Kumbhojkar textbook.'

'Forget it! He didn't take your attendance, right?' I asked him.

'No he didn't.'

We left. It was our first mass bunk in engineering. Mass bunking is always a challenge. It is not so easy to stop the nerd students from attending a lecture. *These students probably have the same blood group as the professors,* I thought. But we had been able to convince them today. A proud feeling came over me, like I had my engineering degree in hand.

We were telling everyone from the other section that we had managed our first mass bunk.

Due to mass bunking, we were given four assignments by the professors of each subject. Swapnil and I decided to bunk the classes and write the assignments. Anup too joined us. Rohit had done the assignments already. We took his papers and left the class. I decided to call Sameer and asked him to join us. He did not have any assignments though. But bunking classes was always fun. We decided to sit at the local Aerol railway station. It was the best place to play cricket, or have a nice time with your girlfriend, or even write assignments for that matter. The last one we hardly did, though. The frequency of trains was one after almost two to three hours. So it was always a vacant platform like any other Navi Mumbai platform. The station was hardly 5 minutes away from our college and we reached there in no time. There were hardly any people on the platform and we spotted very few students. Some couples were sitting hand in hand. We had four assignments to be written. The writing work commenced. Sameer soon got bored waiting for us and broke the silence.

'So you guys were yourselves interested in engineering or were you forced to take it up by your parents?' Sameer asked Swapnil and Anup.

'I was always interested in engineering. I wanted to be an IT engineer. It offers you a white collar job. I love that kind of lifestyle. What about you?' Swapnil replied.

'Same here. Even I wanted to be a civil engineer. It gives you an opportunity to earn more than other categories of engineers. A civil engineer gets the desired salary as white income, but along with that lots of black money can also be earned,' he winked.

'Is money everything?'Anup asked.

'No. But we need money for everything, don't we? If we need to drink water, we need money. If we need food, money is required and so on. What better field than engineering to provide for our monetary needs? Moreover, being a civil engineer is like sone pe suhaaga,' Sameer laughed.

'What about you Anup?' I asked.

'Kya yaar…why are you thinking so much? All of us have got admission. Now we cannot change things. Whether we like it or not, we have to get our asses fucked for four years. Ab lag Gaye la**e. So stop this discussion and start writing assignments. Or else Deshmukh sir will cut our dicks into pieces,' said Anup in all seriousness.

His speech made me feel good. I felt as if I was not alone and somebody thought like me. Who can be forced to do this bullshit, anyway? I really felt at that time that engineering was like marriage. Bachelors are eager to do it. But married people declare themselves dead a few years into the marriage.

After writing assignments and having lunch on the platform itself, we started walking towards college. Anup saw a 'Tapri' near college and asked us to join him. I was unaware that Anup smoked.

'Anup, smoking kills…' Swapnil said.

'Ya, but slowly,' he replied.

I loved his cocky reply. The want in me to smoke was increasing each second. I had never tried smoking before, though Sameer had. Anup and Sameer kept forcing me to give it a try.

'Have it, yaar. It's nothing serious. You will cough slightly in the beginning but then when you get used to it, you'll feel normal. Plus, cigarettes keep your mind active. You think better. So have one puff,' said Anup forcing me.

Finally, I asked him to buy a cigarette for me.

'Bhaiya ek Gold Flake do,' he said to the chacha at the tapri. He handed one to Anup who gave it to me. I took the cigarette in my hand. I was holding one for the first time and it felt something different. Something I had never felt before. There I was, smoking a cigarette with my good friends. Five minutes later, I was expertly blowing out rings.

A cigarette is the only consumer product which, when used as directed, kills its consumer.

And I was ready to be killed. Slow poison, so why to worry? Enjoy it while it lasts. And I did precisely that. I started smoking another cigarette. When we heard that the college would be closed due to heavy rains, we started making plans for the day. Sameer suggested we go to the nearby waterfall and we agreed.

Since it was at a short distance, we decided to walk towards the destination. All four of us were enjoying in the rains. Sameer had bought three bottles of beer along and we went and sat close to waterfall. It was an awesome view. I did not drink. I had never tried it before. Not even on that day. I had taken three cigarettes with me. I was enjoying the moment with a cigarette in my hand. Everyone was drunk. It became difficult for me to control them. However, I was enjoying their silly drunk jokes. It was the first time all four of us had gone out and enjoyed together.

Sameer—though he had a few bad habits, he was sincere. I knew friends like him were rare to find. He helped me whenever I needed him and had helped me many times before. I cherished our friendship.

Swapnil—he was a new friend. A frank guy with an X-factor which I couldn't quite decode. He was a charmer and I knew he could bring many girls close to me. This is the quality of a true friend.

Anup—I really could not understand him. Though we had become friends, he always seemed aloof and lost in his own world. He never came too close to us. He was transparent in his proceedings but there was something missing in him.

Our First Meeting

We were living in our own little world. A world of fun and enjoyment. I had never thought life in an engineering college could be so much fun. Moreover, I didn't think I would manage to get such wonderful friends. Still I thought something was missing. Girls. We used to sit on the last bench and observe the girls in our class. It was the first lecture of the day.

'Look at the girl in second row in a blue T-shirt. She is so hot,' Swapnil whispered in my ears.

'No yaar, she just has a pretty face. Look below her neck. They aren't even the size of carrom coins.'

'Hmmm…maybe you are right,' Swapnil admitted.

'What about the girl in black in the third row. How is she?' Swapnil continued.

'Not my type. You can try your luck with her.'

We stopped the discussion and began paying attention to the lecture. Five minutes into the lecture, a girl shouted from the back door, 'May I come in sir?'

I looked at her and my heart skipped a beat. Was I watching a dream? She was no Angelina Jolie, but there was something about her that made my heart skip a beat. I asked myself, *Is she the one I am looking for?*

She came and sat in the third row. Once settled, she turned to look behind her. Our eyes met for a fleeting second and I felt like our souls had united. Somewhere in my heart I knew she was the one for me. After a while, I started giggling and she gave me the most incredible smile I have ever seen. I felt something I had never felt in my life before——true love. I had heard that love was that tingly feeling inside you when you get a call or message from your partner. You smile and your heart beats a thousand times a minute! Love is, when you hold your partner's hand, and know that there is nothing better in the world than being with that person.

But nothing like this happened here. I think I just felt attracted to her because of her looks. Her dress. Her eyes. Her lips. I told myself it was purely lust and nothing else. Love can't happen in a second. But it wasn't just lust either. I was thoroughly confused.

A week passed and I still couldn't get her out of my mind—the way our eyes met for the first time and the incredible smile she gave me. My attitude in class had changed. I wanted more of her attention. My dressing style changed. I became more conscious of how I looked. I just wanted to talk to her somehow but was afraid. It was not that tough to talk to her but I didn't know the right way to make the first move. I knew she was keeping an eye on me. I knew that in her heart she liked me too. But I was afraid. This was happening to me for the first time. I had had many girlfriends before. But this was something different. This was like rains in the summer. This was like shining sun in clouds.

♋♋

A few days later, I headed for the computer practicals. We entered the lab. I took the computer in the corner. Swapnil was sitting beside me. She entered the lab. She was looking awesome in a red top and low waist dark blue jeans. Her top was somewhat transparent and her sexy shape attracted me. It made me more nervous. She came and sat besides Swapnil. We were asked to write the experiment from the manual. Swapnil was looking at my nervous face. I was looking at her on the sly. And I knew she was doing the same. There was something odd between us. I watched her lips closely. Soft and luscious. Was I falling for her?

Swapnil exchanged a few words with her. I was getting jealous watching them talk. Swapnil was fast in chatting up girls. I still did not know her name and he was talking to her as if he had known her for the past few years. Even I wanted to join the conversation. But something stopped me.

The professor started with the roll call. Now was my chance to know her name.

'Roll no. 33.'

'Present, Ma'am,' she replied.

Shit! Chance gone. She responded so quickly that I missed her name. We left the lab and I hurriedly went upto Swapnil and asked him her name. He told me it was Riya.

Riya and Aditya…made for each other?

Swapnil started talking to her regularly day after day in class or through SMS chats. Even Anup had been conversing with her. It was just me who was left now.

When we were leaving for home after college, I asked Swapnil to give me a Xerox of the mechanics assignment given earlier that day. He said he did not have it, and neither did Anup. Swapnil went and asked Riya for the assignment. Finally, she broke the long silence between us.

'I have not written just one question. The rest is all here,' she said handing over the assignment to me.

I was blank. I could not reply. I was just watching her lips move. She was staring back at me.

'Hello, is it okay? I have not written the last question,' she said again.

'Absolutely. No problem. Give me your number. If I have any doubts I will call you.'

Fuck! This is silly, I said to myself. What doubts will I have? But it was too late.

'Okay fine. Take it,' she said writing something on a piece of paper.

'Thanks, bye.'

I had really started loving her for I was continuously thinking of her. The feeling of love, the feeling of romance, the feeling of being together—it was all so overwhelming. I loved her. I really did. I was sure it was love. I tried to ask myself why I loved her. Was it the sway in her hips? Or the colour of her lips? Or was it the love in her eyes, the softness of her skin, the silky hair? I had fallen into her trap, and there was no way out.

I finished writing the assignment. I was staring at her name on the upper right side of the page. I was madly in love. I searched for a nice SMS on my cell to forward to her.

Two difficult things to say in life:
1. HELLO to a person who is unknown
2. GOOD BYE to a person whom you love the most. Good night.

After 15 minutes, my phone buzzed. I opened my Inbox. It was an SMS from her:

Good night. Sweet dreams.

I was excited at the prospect of an SMS chat with her. But I didn't reply. I did not want to show that I was desperate for her. I wanted her to text me. But she didn't. I checked my mobile every 10 or 15 minutes. But it did not show anything. I put the cell on vibration mode and kept it under my pillow in case her SMS came. It had been a few minutes but I still did not get a reply. I felt like I should have replied earlier.

Now it was too late to do so. I cursed myself and went to sleep.

✌✌

Soon the lectures turned interesting. Not because I started loving engineering, but because I started loving her. The way she used to look at me during lectures. The way she used to give me naughty smiles indicating she liked me. Canteen became a regular hangout spot for us. She used to sit beside me in the canteen. We started chatting regularly through SMS. We started calling each other daily. We started sharing our food daily. It was a new world altogether. And I loved each moment of it. We bonded with each other quickly. She too hated engineering and this brought us even closer.

Our assignments, in the meanwhile, had also increased. I was at the station writing an assignment along with Swapnil when Riya called me. I told her to join us. She reached the station within 15 minutes. She lived in Aerol itself. So the station was near her apartment. Swapnil had an inkling that I liked her. I wanted to discuss my feelings for her with Sameer. But he was always busy with his lectures. He hardly bunked any. As we were about to finish our assignments, Swapnil noticed how we were sitting in such close proximity and looking at each other.

He knew we had became more than friends. However our feelings were left unsaid.

'Do you have a boyfriend?' Swapnil asked Riya. I was shocked. I looked at him in anger. Riya looked at me and said with a smile, 'No. I am single.' I did not react.

We started walking towards the college. Swapnil got a call from his dad who wanted him to come to his office immediately due to some personal work which Swapnil didn't disclose. Being left all alone with Riya made me a bit nervous. We had never been alone before. We were always accompanied by either Anup or Swapnil. Sameer hardly came with us. We decided to bunk the lectures and go to a restaurant near our college. I wanted to tell her a few things.

We ordered some snacks. I came to know that sweet kachori was her favourite. Paav bhaji was my favourite.

'Riya, have you ever fallen in love?' I asked her summoning up all my courage.

'No.'

'No one?' I asked again.

'I liked many. But I never loved anyone. Maybe I never found anyone who could be perfect for me. What about you?'

'I was in a relationship for a year or so. Actually, it was during my junior college days. I do not know what it was. Was it love or something else? But when we broke up, it did hurt me for a few days.'

'So are you over it now? Or do you still…'

'I am out of it. My friends were very supportive. They helped me a lot.'

'Don't worry, I am with you,' she said.

What does she mean by that? Does she love me? Did she really say that or did I imagine it? I was confused. I wanted to ask her what she meant. However, what would she think? Would she be okay with it? A million thoughts were running through my mind. Finally, I asked her.

'What do you mean you are with me?' I asked.

'I meant as a friend I am with you always. What did you think?'

'I thought you meant more than a friend. Are you sure you meant that?'

'Yes. I'm sure. Now let's leave,' she said sensing the awkwardness.

'I don't think so. If you want to support me, then you will have to take care of me like a little kid.' I wanted an answer.

'Are you crazy? I'm not your wife.'

'So what? You can take care of me. Can't you? And wow, that is a good word. From now onwards, I will call you my wife.'

'Oh no, please don't. I will take care of you but don't call me your wife. Please.'

I was sure she liked me. I continued flirting with her.

'I will call you my wife. In addition to that, you have to take care of me. Like a little kid. Like your sweet bachcha. Is that okay?'

'Do whatever you want,' she blushed.

We left for our respective homes. I had had the best time of my life till date. Shortly afterwards, I got a message from her saying that it was the best time she ever had. That made me love her more.

That night before sleeping, I sent her a long SMS.

Hey dear, oops sorry, my dear wife. This was the best day of my life. Talking to you makes me feel complete. Looking into your eyes makes me feel energetic. So much so that I am still missing you, my sweet kachori. My dearest friend. Thanks a lot for spending quality time with a person like me who dosen't even deserve your friendship. Thanks a lot. Miss you, my wife. Take care. Good night. See you tomorrow.

I got an immediate reply.

Good night, my bachcha. My husband. Haha...tc, good night. And don't take these things seriously.

I loved the first part of the SMS. It told myself that someone really cared for me. Someone loved me a lot. Showered me with love and affection. I was overjoyed. But why the hell did she have to write the next part? Girls will be girls. They will never show what is going on in their mind. However, they do not know that boys are much smarter than them. I knew she loved me but didn't have the guts to tell me.

We were slowly coming closer to each other. But she never said she loved me. I tried telling her about my feelings by dropping hints like casually saying 'I love you', but there would be no reaction from her side. I started calling her MY WIFE, something she liked. We started bunking lectures as submissions were getting closer and many write-ups were pending. Swapnil, Anup, and Riya helped me in writing the class assignments as I was lagging behind them.

♌♌

Once we were sitting in the hall of the college. I was talking on phone while Riya was writing my assignment. The sheet she was writing on fell on the ground. So she bent to pick it up. She was wearing a red top and light blue jeans that revealed her shapely figure. As she bent down, her top moved upwards, revealing her back. Her back was just too sexy. I wanted to touch it. I wanted to move my fingers all over it. I purposely stood back and kept watching. I wanted her on bed right there. But I knew she would not have agreed to it and nor was there a bed around. I went close to her from behind. I could feel the fragrance of her body. I could feel her warmth. I wanted to kiss her neck. I went too close. I wanted her. But I wanted our 'first time' to be special. She was my love. I wanted to spend my entire life with her. I wanted her to be my wife. I wanted her to take care of me.

She looked at me. She was surprised to see me so close to her. I bent down and whispered in her ears, 'Pull down your top. It has moved a bit up.'

Before she could realize what had happened, I pulled down her top for her. This was the first time I had touched her. My heart was beating at an abnormal speed. She blushed, but did not say anything. She was too good for me.

The Applied Mechanics practicals began at 2 pm. They were held in a small classroom. I sat with Riya.

Thakur sir was giving a small lecture on trusses. I was not interested in trusses. I was interested in shapes and curves. I was sitting beside my love. My wife.

'When did we marry? Do you remember?'

'Shut up, Aadi. We are in the middle of a practical.'

I used to love it when she would call me Aadi. It made me feel like she loved me too. I really wished she did.

'So what. As if you are learning something productive or as if you have interest in learning about mechanics. Utter bullshit all this is.'

'Aadi, it's a tough subject. We won't be able to clear it if we don't study.'

'Leave it yaar. I have joined coaching classes on Saturdays. Why should we worry? I will teach you.'

'Okay fine. Now tell me what you want to ask?' she replied.

'Do you remember when we got married?'

'Stop trying to be funny. You know we are not married. We are just friends.'

'What yaar!. Let it be. It's better if we concentrate on mechanics.'

She gave me a sweet smile after the discussion which said it all. Maybe she was afraid of accepting that she loved me. I wanted to find out the real reason.

I always wanted to tell her how much I admired her. I always wanted to tell her that whenever she would be upset, I would hold her tight. I always wanted to hang out with her. Play with her hair. Pick her up, tickle her, and wrestle with her. Hold her hand and run. Just hold her hand and kiss her. Give her piggyback rides, Push her on swings. Tell her she looked beautiful. When she was sad, I wanted to stay on the phone with her, even if she was not saying anything. I wanted to look into her eyes and smile. Kiss her on her forehead. I wanted to kiss her in the rain. I wanted to tell her all of this.

We started appreciating each other in every possible way we could. She used to compliment me if I looked nice. I used to do the same for her. I always used to tell her that she looked beautiful in red and black. She use to wear those colours quite often. She liked blue and black on me. Even green sometimes. Sameer, Swapnil, and Anup had taken a backseat in my life. It's not that I avoided them on purpose. However, Riya and I were always in our own dream world. Talking about marriage, teasing each other. It was fun. She never took it seriously though I always did. But I never told her about it.

All my friends started teasing us. They used to say we were 'made for each other'. It was never serious from their side either. I was living the best days of my life. And I had started liking engineering in the process.

One day, we decided to bunk college and just hang out in the canteen. Actually we were not in a mood to sit for lectures. Sameer joined us. We ordered cold drinks and snacks. Riya was looking very beautiful that day in an orange and yellow salwaar kameez. She looked like a perfect wife.

'Let's play a game,' Sameer said.

'Which game? ' I asked.

'Truth or dare. What say?' he asked us. We all looked at each other and agreed to play. Sameer started telling us the rules of the game. We had to sit in a circle and one person would spin an empty cola bottle in the centre. When it stoped, the person in front of whom the bottle's mouth pointed would be given either Truth or Dare. Whosoever got truth would confess something about his life in his own style. And whoever got dare would have to write all the assignments and experiments. The catch was that he would have to write not only his own assignments, but assignments for all of us. The game seemed interesting to me. I had already decided what I was going to do if I chose truth. I wished it was not dare. I didn't want to spend my week writing assignments for the rest.

'Sameer, spin the bottle,' Riya said.

Round and round the bottle went. I wished for the bottle to stop at me. I wanted to do something different.

I was listening to the radio on my phone at the same time. And I had decided whichever song it would play, I would dedicate it to Riya.

The bottle stopped at Sameer. We all decided to give him dare so that he would have to write all the assignments for us. A majority of people in Electronics made Civil suffer. He reluctantly agreed since he had set the rules and couldn't back out.

In the next round, the bottle stopped at Riya. I gave her truth. Now it was her turn to confess. I was waiting for her to say something that could take our relationship to the next level.

'I don't have anything big to confess. I am originally from Borivli, Western Mumbai. I did my schooling there. I shifted here due to my dad's business in Navi Mumbai. Initially it was difficult for me to settle here in Aerol. I had to change my way of dressing. I also have a younger brother named Ameya. I call him bachcha. He is my life. My parents tell me that I have to look after his education later on. Ummm…What else? Yes, I am very possessive about Shah Rukh Khan. I love him a lot. If anyone says anything against him, I get really mad.'

She stopped short and looked at us. All of us started applauding. My respect for her grew even more. Not because she loved Shah Rukh Khan but because she loved her brother so much. She was perfect. She is going to be my wife, I said to myself.

The next time the bottle stopped at me. Swapnil gave me truth. I had already decided what I would do. I just put my earphones on and switched on the radio on my Nokia 2300 mobile phone. I searched all the channels for a nice song and stopped on one.

'I am dedicating this song to Riya...'

Everyone started with ooo's and aaa's and Riya started blushing.

Lagta hai yeh kyun mujhe...sadiyon se chaahun tujhe...
Lagta hai yeh kyun mujhe...sadiyon se chaahun tujhe...
Mere sapno me aake...mujkho apna banaake...
Mujhpe tu kar ehsaan...jiya dhadak dhadak...jiya dhadak dhadak jaaye...

After I finished singing, everyone clapped loudly and Riya gave me a huge smile.

'So sweet of you. You are my best friend. Thanks a lot,' she said happily.

I wanted her to realize how much I loved her. I needed a shoulder to lean on, someone who would listen patiently to all my problems. I wanted her to realize that she was the only girl who excited me. When I was with her, I felt like I was out of control! When I was with her, I felt no fear. I had fallen for her badly.

'Are you in love with her?' Swapnil asked me when we went to order a sandwich.

'Yes, I am in love with her. I am crazy about her,' I replied.

'Then go and tell her. I think she loves you too. I was observing her reaction when you were singing the song.'

'You think so? Maybe she does loves me. But I am not sure. Let's see what the future has in store for us.'

We had snacks. Riya was blushing throughout. This was the first time I saw her blush so much. If I could have just one wish, I would wish to wake up everyday with the warmth of her lips on my cheeks, the touch of her fingers on my skin, and the feel of her heart beating with mine...I was deeply in love. And I was sure this feeling wouldn't come with anyone else but her in future.

❧❧

November 10. The preliminary exams had begun. The first paper was Applied Chemistry. I was blank. I was unaware of what was in the syllabus. Riya's roll no. was 33 and mine was 36. She got a seat in front of me. There were four students in each row. I didn't know answers to even a single question. The professor started distributing papers. I requested Riya to show me whatever she was writing. I just wanted to write something on the answer paper. I was repeatedly reading the same questions over and over again. There were five questions of 10 marks each. I felt as if I was seeing the questions for the first time. I was not surprised. I had never studied earlier. Riya started writing. I was constantly whispering in her ears to show me something. After writing one page, she passed on the paper to me. I started copying whatever she had written. She had answered two questions. I gave her the paper back after sometime. The professor didn't noticed what we were doing. He was busy consuming his tea and samosas. After answering the two questions, I got up to leave. Everyone started smiling as I was leaving barely 20 minutes into the paper.

I went outside the college to chacha's tapri. I lit a cigarette and was thinking about Riya. We had known each other only for a couple of weeks and she already had me completely and totally infatuated. I didn't even want to think about being with anyone else. I thought that if I could keep myself busy, I would be okay. But I was so overwhelmed by my feelings for her. I needed to hear her voice always. I needed to feel her touch. I was madly in love with her. I wanted to tell her that she was everything to me. She was the one for me. I just could not imagine her with anyone else. I was becoming increasingly possessive.

However, I kept thinking to myself, does she think the same way as me? What if she loves someone else? No, she doesn't love anyone. She had said so that day. But what if she is lying? No, she could not lie. I could see the love in her eyes for me. But is it true love? What was it that I saw? What if she rejects me? What if she didn't want anything beyond friendship? I had to know everything. I could not keep waiting like this.

All these thoughts were running in my mind. I left the tapri and started moving towards college. I wanted to shout at the top of my voice, I love you Riya. I can't imagine my life without you. I love you a lot.

A Day to Remember

It was Saturday evening. I was just chilling at home, playing games on my PC. I logged on to Gmail chat. Riya was online.

Me: 'Hi, whats up?'

Riya: 'Nothing special, was just checking my mail.'

Me: 'Some important mails?'

Riya: 'No yaar, just casual ones.'

Me: 'So what's up with my wife? How was her day?'

Riya: 'What wife re! I am not your wife.'

Me: 'You are my wife.'

Riya: 'Tell me one thing seriously, will you?'

Me: 'I will try to.'

Riya: 'Are you ever serious or do you just joke all the time?'

Me: 'Regarding what,the 'wife' thing?'

Riya: 'Yes, exactly.'

Me: 'What you think? Am I joking or am I serious?'

Riya: 'I think you are joking.'

Me: 'Shall I be frank today?'

Riya: 'Yes, I want to know what is going on in your mind.'

Me: 'Okay listen, I am serious. You are my wife.'

Riya: 'Are you kidding again?'

Me: 'No, I am very serious actually.'

Riya: 'I don't think so. Anyway, I gotta go. Bye.'

Me: 'Now what is this? Why are you ignoring the topic and leaving?'

Riya: 'I have to leave. Sorry my husband…haha… Will chat with you on SMS. Bye.'

It made me very angry. Why did she always avoid this topic? Why do girls like to irritate us so much? Why could they not be straightforward? I took my phone and sent her a message.

```
Dear Riya, I am very serious about what I said
and I will shout it from rooftops. I hope you
will not let me down. Coming Monday, I will
tell you something that is in my heart. Okay?
```

I got a message shortly afterwards.

```
It's okay. I will not let you down.
```

I called her up. She was in a bus. She was coming from her class. I asked her if she was serious and wouldn't let me down, or was she taking it lightly as always.

'Aadi, I am serious. I will not let you down. You can say whatever you want to. Even I am serious.'

'Pakka, are your sure? It will be embarrassing for me if you…'

'Don't worry my husband. I will not let you down. Do whatever you want.'

'Are you sure I can do whatever I want in public?' I was flirting.

'Stop being naughty and keep the phone down. Bye,' she said and hung up.

Was she serious? I had made up my mind of proposing to her on Monday. I hoped she would say yes. I was feeling nervous, excited, fearful—all at the same time.

I hoped she loved me too.

Was it going to be the beginning of our relationship?

What would happen if she came to know about my past relationships?. I wanted to tell her that she was not the first girl in my life. Nevertheless, she would be the last girl in my life. I was really amazed by her beauty. The way she used to talk with me. The way she cared for me. The way she used to force me to eat in the breaks. The way she used to send me a sweet good morning SMS. The way we used to talk during nights. Everything was special about her.

That night, I thought of flirting with her on the phone for a bit. It was already 11 pm. But still I messaged her.

Are your legs tired?

Why? came the reply.

Because the entire day you were running in my
mind. Aren't you tired?

Shut up, Aadi…and go to sleep. Miss you. Take
care. Gn. Sd.

She loved me. She surely did. I wanted her to be with
me always. My life had changed ever since she came
into it. I had become more responsible.

I called Sameer and Swapnil in the morning. I asked
them to meet me immediately. I was very anxious to tell
them how things were progressing between Riya and me.

When I told them about every single SMS, they were
not surprised. They knew this was bound to happen.

'So are you serious about her?' Swapnil asked me.

'Yes, this time I am serious. Trust me, I want to
marry her and I will.'

'Did you tell her about your previous relationships?'
Sameer added.

'No yaar, I will tell her on Tuesday itself after mid-
terms get over.'

'Aadi are you really serious about her? She is a very
sweet girl. I treat her like my sister. I will kill you if your
intentions are just to sleep with her,' Swapnil said
raising his voice.

'I am really serious man. Please do not take this the
wrong way. I do not have any wrong intentions. I
would never do anything like that to her. I really love
her a lot. I keep thinking of her all the time. It has

never happened with me before. If it was lust then I would have wanted to just sleep with her and get it done with. But I want her to be my wife for good. Please trust me.'

They both looked at each other and finally smiled and said, 'So what's the plan for tomorrow?'

'I haven't thought about it right now. All I know is I want November 14 to be so special that we remember it for the rest of our lives. I want to show her that I can really keep her happy.'

'Have you asked her about her past?' Sameer asked, concerned.

'No I haven't, but she said during the game in the canteen that she doesn't love anyone. So I did not think of asking her.'

'Aadi it was just a game. Maybe she too was in a relationship earlier.'

'Oh shut up. This can't happen. I know she is beautiful and hot. But I know she won't lie. I trust her.'

We all left after that. During the course of our conversation, we had smoked a total of 10 cigarettes.

November 14. Monday. The day I would get my love. The day which would bring sunshine in my life. I won't be the same Aadi anymore. I would be committed. I would be committed to a girl whom I loved with all my heart. Every boy would want a girlfriend like her. Every man would want a wife like her. I was indeed lucky. I thanked God from the bottom of my heart that I decided to opt for engineering. Otherwise I would have never met Riya.

Just when I was deep in thoughts, I got a message from Riya.

```
Jab achanak unki yaad aati hai,
Dil ki dhadkan rukh jaati hai,
Itni khoobsoorat hai unki aankhein,
Ki unse nazar milte hi,
Hamari nazar jhuk jaati hai.
I want to know what you are thinking right now.
But I will wait. Meet you in college.
```

I replied, `I am waiting for you to respond...`

She replied, `What are you wearing tomorrow? Wear something in green, the colour suits you. What should I wear?`

I replied, `Wear anything dear. You look beautiful in any colour.`

After our brief chat ended, I retired to bed. The next morning, I wore a green shirt and left for college. On the way, I purchased a snow spray and ribbon spray used in birthday parties. I also purchased a red rose. We had a maths paper at 11 am. I was standing on the third floor. I saw her entering the college. My heart skipped a beat. She was looking amazing.

Soon we entered the classroom and the paper started. I left the classroom in 15 minutes and gestured for Riya and Swapnil to leave soon too. I had told Sameer to keep his mobile on vibrate mode so that he could leave the paper as soon as I called him. Within 10 minutes, we were at the gate of our college.

I told everyone that we were going to the garden behind our college. Riya refused to come there. I feared that she was going to reject the proposal. Swapnil convinced her to come along. She finally gave in after much convincing and I told Swapnil and Riya to go ahead. I explained to Sameer what my plan was and handed over the spray to him. I went ahead and asked Swapnil to wait for Sameer as he was the one who would explain to Swapnil what the plan was. Riya and I moved ahead. We reached the garden.

I could feel a sense of fear in Riya's eyes. Even I was a bit nervous.

'What do you want to say? Why have you brought me here?' Riya asked innocently, almost as if she did not know what was happening.

'You know why you are here, don't you?'

'Yes I know it. But I want to hear it from you.'

I had kept the rose in one hand, hiding it from her. She had a mischievous look in her eyes. My heartbeats were increasing with each passing second. I never had this feeling before. Should I go ahead and do whatever I had planned or should I keep it simple? However, I wanted this moment to be special. I looked into her eyes. They told me that she too wanted this moment to be special. Every girl wishes for her guy to propose to her in the best way he can. Riya was no different.

'Ready?' I asked her.

'Yes, go on,' she replied.

I told her to trust me and close her eyes. Swapnil and Sameer were standing in one corner, ready with what I had told them to do. I bent down on my knees, kept the rose in my hand and said, 'You are my best friend. A friend like you is hard to get. However, a life partner like you for a person like me is impossible.'

She opened her eyes and looked at me.

'Really, I don't deserve a girl like you. I am a flirt, I have the worst image, but still I want to change. I want to improve. I want a girl who can improve me. And it's you my bachcha. I know you are the one and only, you are my everything. You are the love of my life. I love you babe. And every time I see you, I just want to hug you and never let you go. You are special to me. You make me complete. I will never leave you alone in this relationship. Love you. Do you wish to be my beloved?'

She had tears in her eyes. Tears of happiness. She just nodded and said, 'I love you too my bachcha…love you a lot. Thanks for this moment.'

She accepted the rose. I stood up and we hugged each other. As soon as we hugged each other, Sameer started blowing the snow spray and Swapnil blew the ribbon spray.

She was overwhelmed with whatever I had done for her. We hugged each other for some time. We looked into each other's eyes. Her eyes asked me whether I would be with her forever. My eyes replied to her that I was with her—always and forever…

We left the garden holding hands, looking into each others eyes. It was so beautiful. A new life had started. I succeeded in making this moment memorable for a lifetime.

I tried hard to control my feelings, but was falling for her even more with each passing day. I tried to hide my love from her. I tried to convince my heart that she was just a friend. But it was a lie. Deep inside I was falling in love. I tried to avoid looking into her eyes. But I couldn't.

A simple glance turned into a stare. Still I pretended that I did not care.

However, I was with her. I was with my love. I hoped it wasn't a dream. I wanted someone to pinch me. I hoped everything was real. I wanted to shout to the whole world that I was in love.

I called her as soon as I reached home.

'What is my bachcha doing?' I asked her.

'I am making tea for my mom. Then I have to go to the general store. And later I have to help my brother with his homework.'

'Uhhh, packed schedule. Good. What about your husband? Even I want to have tea made by you.'

'Come home then. My mom will give you tea with sweets. After all, her son-in-law would be coming home for the first time.'

'Let it be. Better, I stay at home. You do your work.'

'Miss you. I want to give you a tight hug, you made my day so special. I have made a diary entry of it to cherish it forever. Thanks for everything. It was the best day of my life. I can't get better life partner than you.'

'I am missing you a lot too. You just want to hug me. But I want to do much more to you. I want to kiss you, touch your hair, hug you tight...'

'Stop being naughty on the phone. My mom is around. Love you bachcha. Miss you a lot. Now shall I keep the phone down? I have lots of work.'

'Okay. Bye. Do miss me.'

I could not sleep as I was thinking of her. This kind of love was new to me. It was true love. I had butterflies in my stomach.

I wanted to be with her. I was experiencing the feeling of first love. I was not able to sleep at all. I was unable to concentrate on anything. Whenever I closed my eyes, all our moments together flashed in front of me. I was proud of myself that I had proposed to her in a special way. I had seen many of my friends proposing but I had never seen anyone doing something like this. It was something unusual and unique. We did not get time to hang out somewhere, but even the little time spent with her, holding her hands and looking at her, staring at her, was special. I was realizing what love was, why people used to say falling in love is always wonderful. I was feeling it today. You may achieve everything in your life—money, status, power, everything—but it could not overcome the happiness of what it was to be with the one you loved.

❧

November 16. Mid-terms had come to an end. We decided to go out somewhere. It was our first date as a couple. We did not plan for it though. We decided to go to a shopping mall. We left college as soon as we finished our last paper. We were waiting for the train at Aerol station. Swapnil and Sameer were at the station itself.

'See how friends change when they get a girlfriend,' Swapnil said to Sameer jokingly.

'Oh come on, Aadi has not changed. I told him to leave immediately after the paper,' Riya replied.

'So now you have started taking his side? Very good.'

'Stop it yaar, Swapnil. We are going to a mall.'

The train came and we left. Riya was not used to train journeys. She stood close to me and held my hand tightly. I loved the fragrance of her body. I was showing her the poster in the train that had the names of the stations of central railways. She gave me a confused look. It made me smile. She did not care about the world. All she cared for was me. I felt special to have her in my life. We had to catch another train to reach our destination. She did not like train journeys. I could see it in her eyes.

'Bachcha, 5 minutes and we will reach,' I assured her and she came and stood closer to me.

'This is frustrating. We could have come by rickshaw,' she said, disgusted with the huge crowd that left no room for us.

'Leave it now, we are about to reach Mulund.'

Mulund was a crowded station. We caught a rickshaw to reach R Mall. We were carrying a folder in our hand which had all the assignments and experiments. I kept it behind the seat in the rickshaw. I came closer to her and put my hand on her shoulder. She blushed.

'Love you.'

'Love you too,' she replied. I could never get tired of hearing her say this. It made me realize that this was not a dream.

I came closer to her. There was hardly any distance between us now. We were both staring at each other. There was complete silence. A sense of fear. A sense of love. Her eyes spoke a lot. They told me how much she loved me. She whispered the same in my ears and closed her eyes. Our relationship was moving so quickly that it had been just two days since I proposed to her and here we were sitting so close in a rickshaw that hardly any air passed between us. I was about to kiss her. Kiss her in public. I couldn't have cared less about the onlookers. We were deeply in love and nothing else mattered.

Her eyes were closed. I went closer to her. I remembered Nikita…

Will she be a better kisser than Nikita? Nikita was hot. More experienced may be. What if even Riya is experienced? I did not care. I loved her. However, she had never told me anything about her previous relationships.

My hand was resting gently on her cheek, while my fingertip slowly moved down her neck. She was breathing heavily, a sign of nervousness. As I was listening to the sound of her breath, her hand slowly began to move up along my back. I felt the movement of her cheek. I began to inch towards her. My heart began to beat faster, and the closer I got, the more nervous I became. My hand moved around to the back of her neck and into her hair. As I reached her, I could hear my heartbeat echoing throughout my head. I pushed back and my cheek came to rest on hers. I was disappointed with myself, but she turned her head towards me, gently encasing my bottom lip between hers. My fear instantly dissipated and I kissed back, leading to the most romantic embrace. Our lips met. Our first kiss that lasted until we reached the mall. It was out of the world. I was a fool to compare her with Nikita.

'Please don't leave me ever,' said Riya after the kiss ended.

'No my jaan, I won't leave you. I cannot live without you now. I cannot get anyone better than you. In fact, I do not want anyone better than you. Love you so much.'

We got down from the rickshaw. The driver gave us a strange look. Maybe he was watching whatever was happening from the rearview mirror. However, I couldn't be bothered about it. It was my first kiss to my love.

We entered the food court of the mall. I ordered my favourite—paav bhaaji. We decided to share it. Riya dipped the paav into the bhaaji and fed me with her own hands. It was an out of the world feeling. Riya was looking more beautiful when she was feeding me. My love for her was increasing day by day. Romance was in the air. Each moment with her was like whiskey. The more time I spent with her, the more I went out of my senses.

'Aadi... let's watch a movie.'

'Now? Its already 3.30 pm. Won't you be late for home?'

'I will make an excuse. Now come on, let's go. Please.'

'Okay, let's check the movie timings.'

We went to R Adlabs. There was only one show in the next one hour.

'Are you sure you want to watch this movie?' I asked.

'Yes, let's buy the tickets.'

The show was for 3.45 pm, the movie was *Tajmahal,* and the hall number was Screen 2.

I wondered what went on inside these girls' heads. Maybe they just wanted to spend some quality time with us. But *Tajmahal* was too much for me to bear. But for her sake, we went into the theatre.

The movie soon started. I completely ignored the movie and just glanced at the innocence in Riya's eyes.

'How much do you love me?' she asked.

'A lot,' I said.

'I love you more than that,' she replied.

I took her hand in mine and kissed it. She gave me a smile. We just kept looking at each other. Throughout the movie we were engrossed in cosy moments like these. I could sense the fear and excitement in her. She was bold and sweet at the same time. Very rarely does a girl have both qualitites. I was lucky to have them in Riya. We did not exchange a single word but our eyes said it all. As the lights were on, we realized the movie was over. I hadn't seen one scene in the movie.

'What will you tell your friends? That we watched *Tajmahal*? And if you say so dear, what story are you going to tell them?' I teased her.

'Shut up,' she said blushingly.

'I really love you a lot. Always be with me.'

We smiled and as we left the mall, I realized I had left the folder in the rickshaw. We were so engrossed in each other that I had totally forgotten that I had kept the folder behind the seat.

'Jaan, I left the folder in the rickshaw!' I told her.

'What? Are you serious? You are so dumb yaar. Now what?'

'I don't know. We have lost it. What should we do now?' I was worried.

'You screwed everything up, man! You should have realized it earlier, at least.' She was looking at me furiously.

'Now what?'

'We have to write it again and submissions are barely six days away. How will we complete so many write-ups? How could you forget it?' She was almost on the verge of tears.

'Don't worry, jaan. I will write everything—for you and for me. Don't worry. You are such a passionate kisser that I forgot everything. I could only feel your lips.'

'Can you be serious once in your life Aadi?'

'Okay fine. I am seriously telling you that I will handle it. Trust me.'

But deep down I was worried. How will I be able to write so much in such a short span of time? If I had shown my nervousness, she would have started crying. I did not want to make her upset. But what next? There are five subjects and each subject has almost 7 to 8 write-ups. That meant almost 35 write-ups. Moreover I said I would write Riya's write-up also. That made it 70. Impossible. I was screwed. Why on the earth did I have to keep it behind the seat?

I went with her to drop her home by bus. She was worried and I could see it. I tried to make her laugh and smile by reminiscing about all our memories from the day we met for the first time. She finally smiled.

After leaving her home, I boarded the bus back to my home. Along the way, I kept thinking to myself how submissions were going to be the worst. Good start to engineering life, I said to myself.

All that made me happy was that I had met Riya. Nothing else. 70 write-ups in 5 days.

Too Close, Too Fast

Lectures were over and we were given a study leave or PL as we called it. But I still had to give the submissions. It was already mid-November. Exams were declared for December 7. I was writing all the assignments for Riya and me. Riya was also helping me out. We had classes almost every evening. It was difficult for us to meet now since our classes were different. Therefore, we decided to bunk classes and meet in the evenings. The syllabus had been almost covered. Not many important topics remained. We decided to meet in central garden near our class. Not everyday, but every alternate day atleast.

The central garden was one of the most famous grounds in central Mumbai. During the daytime, kids played cricket and football. Mostly cricket. And it became a lover's point in the evening after sunset. Couples used to hang around and sit close to each other. People who used to walk on the roadside could not see anything on the ground clearly due to the darkness.

That allowed couples to indulge in anything they wanted.

We decided to meet there at around 6.30 pm. She came by rickshaw from Aerol, Navi Mumbai. She was wearing a black top that revealed her cleavage and a long white skirt. I was blown away by her outfit. She gave me a naughty smile. We went to the ground and we sat there and talked. I asked her about her family and where she had studied earlier.

'Ameya, my brother, studies in St. Xavier's, Aerol. He is currently in class 7. We shifted here a few years back due to my father's business. I do not have many friends here, just three to four, out of which one is from our college. The rest are from my neighbourhood. Actually I really hate staying in Aerol. But I do not have any other option. I got admission in this college through management quota. It's a boring life here in Aerol. Western Mumbai was much better. We used to have lots of fun there. All my friends are there. We used to go shopping, watch movies, and had an awesome life there. But due to dad's business in Navi Mumbai we had to shift.'

'Okay. Then I must thank your dad for taking the decision to settle here in Aerol. If he had not taken that decision, we would not have been sitting together like this.'

She smiled and I kissed her forehead. She asked me about my family.

'I have one sister, Ketki. She is very sweet. We have the same bonding that you share with your brother. My family is very frank with me. My dad is an engineer and works on ships. He stays away for 2 months and then is on leave for 2 months. My mom works in a government office. It's a normal life. Nothing special. Nevertheless, I love my family a lot. They mean a lot to me.'

'Do you smoke?' she asked me.

'Sometimes. Not a chain smoker. To be frank, I smoked my first cigarette around two months back with Sameer and Anup. I had never smoked before that. I don't drink though.'

'You never told me that you smoke. You should have told me.'

'Jaan, I don't smoke regularly.'

I went close to her. I kissed her on the lips. Maybe it was the right time to kiss her to avoid a fight on smoking. It was better than the first kiss. This time it was more passionate. It was dark. No one around. I looked around and saw the place vacant. She held me closely as I kissed her. She opened two buttons of my of shirt and slipped her hands inside. It brought shivers down my body. My hands went inside her top and squeezed her breasts. She moaned in pleasure. I really thought our relationship was moving too fast. Six days after the proposal and we were at the centre of the ground in the dark. Was it a decent thing to do?

But I was enjoying it so much that I didn't care. I continued cuddling her, kissing her. She put her tongue deep inside my mouth.

'Jaan, go easy. We are in a public space,' I cautioned.

'I want to give you a love bite which is visible to everyone so that other girls will know that you're taken and that they should stay away from you.'

'Why will a girl come close to me? I am always with you. How can I go to someone else?'

'Still I want the world to know that you are mine. Just mine. And no one can get you now. I love you. Love you a lot. You are my kid. My bachcha. My Mr Perfect.'

'Okay jaan. Then let me give you a love bite too.'

I gave her a bite below her neck until she moaned in pleasure.

'Now no one will come close to you too. I can't see you with someone else. Please never ever leave me. I am all yours now.'

After some time, we left for home. I had my dinner and I called her up.

'Hey, let's meet tomorrow at the same time. We won't go to class, alright?.'

'Aadi... do you want to fail and get a KT?' In Mumbai University, if we fail in one subject, we call it a KT, i.e. 'keep term' where we are given the option of reappearing in the failed exam.

'No I want you. I will wait for you.'

I hung up. I knew she would come. She never let it show that she needed me but I knew. She was wearing my favourite red top and skirt. We had pani puri and sat on the ground like the previous day. She was driving me crazy with her touch. I was rolling my fingers all over her body. She told me she had worn bikini panties underneath her skirt. I had told her once that it was my fantasy to see her in them. But I did not cross my limits. It was not the right time.

'Is this your first time with a girl?'

I could feel myself getting aroused. What was going to happen next? She was not the first girl I had touched. Should I tell her the truth or should I hide it?

'What happened bachchu, answer me?'

I somehow took control of my nerves and said 'no'. She gave me a big smile.

'What happened?' I asked her.

'I knew it jaan. The way you touched me. The way you kissed me. I knew I was not the first girl in your life.'

'I wanted to tell you this on the first day. But I never got a chance to do so. You are right. You are not the first girl in my life. But I never crossed my limits with any girl. Trust me'

I hoped she would trust me. I was afraid of losing her.

'Yes, I do trust you. I am not fighting with you, I am not upset. I knew this the very first day when you kissed me. But I thought you would tell this to me someday yourself. But you didn't.'

'Sorry jaan, I thought I might lose you. And I can't afford to lose you. I am really sorry.'

She smiled and hugged me. I almost cried at that moment. She kissed my eyes. I could not believe she loved me so much that she forgave me in a few minutes. I had started loving her more. I gave her a sweet kiss on her cheeks.

'Can I ask you one thing?'

'Yes,' she said.

'You said you knew I was with a girl earlier by the way I kissed. But how? If I am the first person in your life, how did you know these things? I mean the kiss must have been your first time too. Then how could you...'

'Who said you are the first? I never said that, jaan.'

'You mean you were in a relationship earlier? But during the truth or dare game, you had said that you loved only your brother. Am I right?'

'I didn't want to open up in front of everybody, but yes, I've been in a relationship before in junior college. It lasted for just 4 months. He was a Christian. I never liked his family. I do not know the reason why he broke up with me. But I do not care now. I love you and nothing else matters.'

I was thrashed. I was broken into pieces when I heard her say this. She had lied to me.

I hadn't done anything different. I had lied too. I just didn't tell her I had been in a relationship before.

Did it mean I was not the first person to touch her? Did it mean I was not the first person to slip my hand in her top? Or did it mean she would leave me too? I did not care if someone had touched her. I loved her and that was enough for me. I loved her more than anything else in the world. But I still felt she should have told me.

'Don't worry, jaan. I will always be with you. I will never leave you,' I said.

She put my head in her lap. I tried to think about our present and future. I smiled at her and kissed her eyes. Our relationship had turned even more pure than before. Now everything was transparent. I was happy she had told me the truth. I was also a little upset because I couldn't imagine seeing her with someone else. I just loved her too much. We did not speak a word and left just looking in each other's eyes. Our relationship had moved one step ahead though I still felt it was moving forward too rapidly. Now I couldn't live without her. But there was one question I still wanted an answer to but didn't know how to ask—Was she really a virgin? What if she was not? Would it affect my love for her?

I don't think so! It was more than just virginity now. We had shared an emotional bonding with each other.

After a few minutes together, we left for our respective homes. As soon as I reached home, I got the best possible SMS from her.

I love the way you look at me, your eyes so naughty and mischievous.

I love the way you kiss me, your lips so soft and smooth.

I love the way you make me happy, and the way you show your care for me.

I love the way you say, 'I Love you',

And the way you are always there. I love the way you touch me, always sending chills down my spine. I love that you are with me, and glad that you are mine... I will never leave you my bachcha...

Does a mother ever leave her child alone? You are my cute little bachcha. I am missing your touch. I am looking at the love bite in the mirror. I wish it was permanent. You are very sweet. I am missing your kiss. I want to get close to you. You rock. I wonder why I met you so late in life. Anyways you are mine. Forever now. And dare you leave me. Miss you...muauaahhh...

Love you too, I messaged back.

She would always tell me to send her a long SMS that she could read again and again when I was not around. But I could never write long messages.

She sent me a reply saying: I want a long SMS. Otherwise I won't talk to you.

Girls are beyond my comprehension. They need to have whatever their heart desires. If we don't listen to them, they start with their emotional drama. I had to do it. I had no other option left. I opened my inbox and searched for a love SMS. I got one that was good enough to be sent. I started editing it as per my requirement. I added a few things and sent it to her. That made her really happy. She did not even realize it was a forwarded SMS. Girls are so foolish. But we boys love them as they are. I did love her a lot. And I was willing to to do anything to make her smile. One cute SMS had made her happy. It said,

```
Many a times we lose our special ones because
we are unable to tell them how special they
are. This SMS is especially to tell my special
one that you are the best thing that ever
happened to me. I never want to lose you. You
are the one who makes me shiver every time you
touch me.
    Every night I stay up late to talk to you.
I love you a lot jaan. And I can honestly say
it will remain like this foreever. Miss you.
Love you. Muaah...
```

'Aadi... wake up. Some rickshaw driver is here to see you,' mom said waking me up.

'What rickshaw driver?' I asked.

I then rememberd the rickshaw driver in whose auto I had lost my folder. I got up quickly and went to the hall. He was sitting there having a cup of tea. I thanked him for his kindness. I saw my folder and then realized Riya had written her name on it as well.

Riya Aditya.

Moreover, she had written her cell number on it. The driver said he had called her up on that number and she had given him my address. I was so glad to see my folder. I had written just 20 assignments until now. But Riya's number had saved us.

In all this process, I had forgotten all about mom! She wanted to know who Riya was and why her name was on my folder. I really hoped the driver had not told her anything about that day. About whatever we had done in the rickshaw. After having a cup of tea, he left.

'Who is Riya? Why is her name on your folder?'

'Mom, she is my friend and she is slightly mad. She does all these sort of silly things. She wrote her name and cell number just for fun.'

'Don't tell me she is just a friend. If she is just a friend, what were you doing with her in the rickshaw?'

Oh my God! I was gone. I was numb. I did not know what to say. Did that driver tell my mom what we did? Bloody idiot! It would have been better if I had to write 50 more assignments than face this scene.

'I did nothing.'

'You went with her to R Mall. Why? What's going on between the two of you?' mom asked angrily.

'Wait, I am calling her right now,' mom said. She took her cellphone and dialled her number.

I wanted to send her an SMS saying don't pick up, but I could not. What will be Riya's reaction? I hoped my mom wouldn't get angry with her. What will she think about my mom?

'Hello, this is Aditya's mom. Thanks beta for telling that rickshaw driver the address.'

I wish I could hear what she was saying. I was carefully observing the expressions on my mom's face.

'What were you two doing in R Mall? Just the two of you?'

If I had consulted an astrologer, he would have surely said I would die in 10 minutes. This was unreal man.

'Are you sure there is nothing between you two?'

No way. No way could I survive. I was sure Riya would have panicked.

'This should not happen again. Okay. Bye.'

What should not happen again? Did she mean kisses? Did she mean we should never be alone together? I wanted to call Riya to enquire what had happened. What had she told my mom?

'I dare you to repeat this thing again. Grow up and concentrate on studies. Exams are only 20 days away.'

'I know, mom. Please don't irritate me. I know what to do and what not to do.' I went into my room and called up Riya.

'Hey, what happened? What were you saying to my mom?'

'Don't worry jaan. Why do you get tensed so easily? Chill, yaar. I have handled everything. I told her we were not alone in R Mall. We went alone but our friends were waiting for us in the mall. I reached the station late and because I didn't know the address, you waited for me and we reached the mall together. Okay? Now smile. Love you.'

'Oh God! You saved me. I thought you would panic. You are the best. How can you be so good all the time?'

'It's your love which makes me good all the time. Miss you. See you in college. Wait near Priyanka Hotel. I will reach around 10.45 am, okay? Bye'

We had to reach college by 11 pm to get our few assignments checked. We did it in an hour or so and I asked Riya where to go.

'Let's go to Grant Lane, Vashi. It will be fun. I will show you a nice place. Mini Chowpatty. Even I have not gone there. Only heard of it. Let's give it a try.'

'Hmm…Ya lets go by bus.'

We started walking towards the bus depot. It was in sector 4, not far from my college. She had made fried rice for me. I must say she is a superb cook.

We got a seat to sit in the bus. Grant Lane was about 15 kilometres away from college. As the bus left the depot, I told her to open her lunch box. I was desperate to have something cooked by her. She started feeding me with a spoon.

'Liked it?'

'Jaan, you are awesome. You are an angel. My pari. You can do anything in this world. Can't you?'

'No, I can just love you and that is more than enough for me,' She said playing with my hair.

'Why do you love me so much? Am I really worth it?'

'Yes sweety, you are the only person worthy of it. I also don't know why I love you. But I really care for you. I love to be with you. I love to play with your hair. I love the way you look at me. The innocence in your eyes brings me closer to you. You have a nice heart. You do not hide any thing from me. You are honest. I love this. And the way you proposed to me, I can never forget that in my life.'

'Can anyone propose to you like I did?'

She did not say anything. She just came close to me and gave me a sweet kiss on my neck. That said it all. No one could separate us now. Colours mixed once cannot be separated again. Our relationship was like those colours. It could not be separated.

❧♡♡❧

We reached Grant Lane, Vashi depot. We got into a rickshaw. Mini Chowpatty was hardly 5 minutes away. It was a quiet place. We had come to this place for the first time. We saw a few couples and some boys playing there. It was all very romantic.

It was a big area. It had a lake. That's why I thought it was called Mini Chowpatty. It had two gardens in front of the lake. They were well maintained. They had nice places for couples to sit. There were trees at the back and a nice lawn. We saw small huts at the back of the lakes. It was far away still we could see couples hanging out in those huts. It was really a romantic place. We loved it. There was a stall of Chinese food also. I found the place the best one to hang out with a girlfriend. Moreover, there were no street boys who passed lewd comments at women. Therefore, it was not a cheap place either. The biggest advantage was there were no residential buildings beside it.

'Riya, this is an awesome place. We will come here regularly. What you think? Do you like it?

'Yes, I love this place. It is so quiet here. So romantic.'

We sat in the garden and looked at the view. I put my head on her lap and slept. She was playing with my hair. I was looking into her eyes and she into mine. She started playing with my eyelids. Each time she touched me, it felt like she was touching me for the first time. It was so sensual. It made me smile. She kissed me on my forehead. I was really enjoying each moment with her. I wanted to give her all the happiness that I could. I was satisfied with my life after meeting Riya. I never realized when I fell asleep.

When I woke up, she was still looking at me and stroking my face. 'Jaan, when did I doze off? Why didn't you wake me up?' I got up and sat beside her.

'I was looking at you. You slept for almost 20 minutes. And I lived my life in these 20 minutes looking at you. I can tell you where each small black spot is on your face and on your neck. You look so cute when you sleep. Therefore, I did not wake you up. Love you.'

'Love you too.'

For some strange reason she used to like my neck. She would always kiss it. She used to put her hand around it gently and say it was hers. Only she had the right to touch it. 'What's there to like in it?' I would ask her. But she never told me the reason. I knew she was different from other girls. Crazy is the right word.

'Riya.I am going to teach you computer programming now'

'Aadi…please….I don't want to study now. I want to talk to you. Please Aadi.'

'Stop it Riya. Exams are getting close and this subject is a little tricky.'

I forced Riya to sit on the grass and open her books. She never loved studying. Nobody does. Even I did not. But we had to study since exams were getting closer. I started teaching her the basics of programming— command, directories etc. After explaining the same concept to her a dozen times, she would still say she had not understood a word. But I wouldn't give up until I had taught her a few basic things.

Since it was late in the evening, we decided to come home by train instead of bus since that was a safer option. It was already 8 pm. Riya got down from the train at Aerol and I continued my journey back home.

Each day with her was like honey. Sweeter and sweeter. I never thought I could love anyone so much.

When I reached home, I was greeted by an angry mother on the door.

'Why are you so late? Were you with Riya?' mom asked me angrily.

'Mom, I had told you I had class. Didn't I?

'I thought you bunked and went to the Mall.'

'Mom you are too much. Give me something to eat now and let me sleep.'

How do mothers know everything about their sons? I couldn't hide anything from her. My eyes and expressions would say it all. However, somewhere I knew she liked Riya.

Sleepless Nights

Submission time is the worst time in engineering. It gets worse if your attendance is low. I knew my attendance was low in Chemistry. I had to submit two experiments as well. I was worried as to what would the response of the teacher be when she came to know about my attendance and experiments. She anyway did not have a good impression about me.

By the time I reached college, the submissions had started. I went to the Chemistry teacher and told her about my status in the subject.

She smiled and said, 'No problem child, its okay. Come next year for submission. Why you want to do it so early. Enjoy yourself for a year and then come for submissions.'

I almost had tears in my eyes. I requested her to accept my submissions. However, she was firm in whatever she said. Riya too was not with me. She was busy with her submission elsewhere. I wanted her near me. Her support meant a lot to me. I called her up. She was busy in the BEE lab. I was standing outside the Chemistry lab waiting for the teacher's opinion to change. But she remained firm in her descision and told me to leave. I left the Chemistry lab and went to give all the other submissions which went off smoothly. Riya had finished her submissions by then.

'Is your submission over?' she asked me.

'No, only Chemistry remains. She is not accepting my file. My attendance is low and I have to check two experiments as well.'

'It's okay. Let me go talk to her. I might be able to convince her to accept your submission after all, she knows me very well.' Saying that, Riya started walking towards the Chemistry lab.

The teacher saw Riya outside the lab and called her inside. I followed her into the classroom.

'Riya, is there any problem?' she asked while writing something on the attendance sheet.

'Ma'am, his experiments are to be checked. Please can you do it?'

'No I won't. Look at his attendance. It's just 42 percent. If it was above 50 percent, I would have thought of it. But as per the rules, it's impossible now.'

I was looking at Riya. She told me to relax.

'Ma'am, please. I promise you he won't repeat this mistake again the next semester. Please ma'am. I give you the assurance he won't repeat this mistake again. If he does, you can cancel my submission.'

'Riya, what's this? You are a nice girl. Why do you hang out with boys like him? '

Bloody hell. What does she mean by that? I would have abused her there itself but I was quiet as I wanted my submissions over. I pleaded with her myself and gave her the assurance that I would be regular in classes for the next semester.

'Riya, I am doing this only for you. You were nice the entire semester and I do not want you to be upset and let that affect your examination. Aditya, you should be thankful to her. Give me your file.'

Finally the submissions was done. I would have screwed my first year if it was not for Riya.

Riya was a sweetheart. I could not have expected more from her. She did what no one else could have done. My first year would have been ruined if Riya had not convinced the Chemistry teacher. She had the power of convincing anyone. I was the best example. Her innocence while explaining things could convince anyone. I had just one word for her— sweetheart.

'Riya thanks, I would have failed if….'

'Just thanks? You owe me a party. Thanks will not do.'

'Okay fine. I don't have cash now. I will treat you after a few days. I will take you to a movie. Is it fine?'

'Yes. Perfect' she said kissing my lips softly.

'Are you crazy? We are in the college.'

I looked around to see if someone had seen us. We were in the passage of the college near the canteen. It was at the back of the college where generally no one came. I was relieved to know that no one was around.

'I don't care. Your lips are mine. I can touch them whenever I want. I don't have to take permission from you.' Riya kissed me again.

I did not argue this time and gave in to her demand.

We went back home. I did not say anything to my parents about my submission. I just went to my room and switched on the computer. Orkutting was my favourite timepass. I used to check Riya's scraps occasionally just to keep an eye on her. I was possessive about her. She was no different. We were happy in each other's company. We did not want anyone to know that we were together.

I remembered I had to take her out for a movie. I checked on the Cinemax website to check which movies were being screened. They were all third-grade. We had decided to watch a movie on Saturday. Till then, I would get some pocket money from my parents.

She came online shortly.

Riya: 'Hey, which movie shall we watch?'
Me: 'Don't know. Let's decide once we reach there. Are you excited?'
Riya: 'Excited? What for? Didn't get you?'

Me: 'Forgot what we did the last time in the theatre?'

Riya: 'Stop it. Love you.'

Me: 'Blushing? I want to see you blushing. Shall I make you blush more?'

Riya: 'No need to see me blushing. How will you make me blush more?'

Me: 'By doing something more than what I did that day. I want you to be just mine. I want you just for me. Even you can do what you want. Love you a lot. Miss you. Eat dinner properly. See you on Saturday. Wear a skirt. If possible, bring fried rice for me.'

I logged out. I wanted the entire day to be special. I was carrying a small gift for her from Archies. I also took a few chocolates for her. I knew how much she loved chocolates.

∾♡♡∾

On Saturday morning, we met outside her house at 11 am. We reached Cinemax in a few minutes. We checked the show timings. There was not even a single good movie. Ultimately, we took the tickets for *Home Delivery*. The show began at 1 pm.

We went to Pizza Hut. I ordered one spicy veggie pizza and a coke.

'Jaan I have two surprises for you. You will love them.'

'Seriously? What are they? Please show me.'

'Not now. You will have to wait for it.' I showed her the packet. She was excited because she loved surprises.

'Even I have one surprise for you,' Riya said pointing at her bag.

It made me so excited that I almost grabbed her bag. But she did not allow me to open it just then. I gave her the wrapped box of chocolates and told her to open it. As she saw chocolates, she pinched my cheeks hard. We shared the first choclate. Then I requested her to show what she had got for me.

She handed a gift-wrapped box to me. I opened it to find that it contained a wrist watch!

'God, this is really nice. From where did you get it?'

'I noticed that you didn't have a watch, so I thought I would get one for you. Thank God you like it.'

'It's your choice. How will I not like it?.'

Even though the watch was not branded, it was such a thoughtful present and showed how much she loved me.

'Now show me what you have with you. Please. I am excited and want to see it.'

'Not now dear. You will have to wait for sometime. But I promise it will be special.'

I wanted to give her that gift just before the movie started. We finished eating our pizza. I paid the bill and we left. There were still 30 minutes left for the movie to start. I asked Riya for her permisiion to smoke. She let me go take a puff. She always used to tell me to smoke within limit. She knew I smoked only occasionally. I went to the tapri, bought a pack, and lit a cigarette. We were sitting outside the theatre.

'Why do you smoke?' she asked me out of the blue.

'Why do you love me?' I asked her back.

'Because you are good looking, good natured, and you know how to make me happy.'

'The same is the case with a cigarette. She looks nice in my hand and she knows how to make me happy.'

She laughed thinking I was joking.

We went inside the theatre. Our seats were in the first row from top. The theatre was almost empty. We had no choice other than to watch this movie. I liked Ayesha Takia as an actress, so did not have any issues. Plus in trailers she had shown her wearing just one white long shirt in a scene. Nothing beneath. That would be exiting to watch. When the movie started, I removed the second surprise from my bag and put it in her hands. Her eyes shone with excitement. She was looking more beautiful than before. She opened it.

'So sweet, it's an awesome ring. Love you a lot. You are the best boyfriend in the world'

I put the ring on her ring finger. She hugged me immediately. It brought tears to her eyes. We had started loving each other to the extreme. She hugged me non-stop for the next 5 minutes. She kissed the ring. It was studded with a diamond. Not a real diamond, obviously. Just a fancy stone that looked like a diamond.

'I will always wear it and whenever I miss you, whenever I am alone, I will kiss this ring. This way, I will always have you near me. Thanks for such a wonderful gift. You are my Mr Perfect. I was right. No one can take your place.'

I kissed her and brought her closer to me. She kissed my chest and neck. I had never seen her as happy as she was today. I started getting naughty with her and so did she. She reached over for some popcorn from the box on my lap and grabbed something else by mistake! Her touch felt good. She was conscious of her mistake but was also eager to see my reaction

After reaching home, she sent me a text.

After today, I am all yours. You must be thinking you gave me two surprises in all, but you actually gave me three. The third one I can't describe it to you, but its always precious for a girl. Think about it and you will realize what I'm talking about. Thanks for everything. I am kissing my ring at the moment. I am missing you more than ever today. It was the most beautiful day in my life. I have saved the date on my mobile. December 3. Love you jaan. Bye. Gn.

After thinking about it for 3 hours, I realized what she meant exactly. This made me love her more. I had taken a chance to propose to her. And today I was deeply in love with her. I could break all boundaries and go beyond my limits. We were made for each other.

It was time for night outs now. Hot coffees, songs on the radio, and some snacks. It was also time to study for the first semester exams. I had never studied earlier except for two subjects. Mechanics and Computer Programming. I was unaware of the syllabus of the other subjects. Exams were 4 days away. The first paper was Applied Mechanics. I had almost prepared for it but I still had to go through it once.

It was around 2 am that I called Riya.

'How much did you study?'

'I am doing the Statics part. It's a tough subject. I think I will get a back. I am sure I'll get a KT,' she replied.

'Don't worry and study. I will not disturb you anymore. Miss you.'

Saying that I kept the phone. I also called Sameer, Swapnil, and Anup to enquire about what they had studied. They were also studying statics. Since I was done with it, I started reading up on dynamics. I found mechanics easy though other students found it difficult.

'So finally are you done with the preparations for the exam? When are you reaching college? I will be there at 10 am. I am so tensed. Let's see what happens,' said Swapnil over the phone.

'I will be there at the same time. Almost done. Let's see.'

I called Riya. Even she had finished studying. The golden figure of '40' was what we all were aiming for.

Thirty minutes before the exam, Sameer was still cramming up. He used to read until the very end.

'Oye topper, close the book,' Swapnil teased him.

'Shut up yaar. I can't remember anything. I am going to screw this paper so badly.'

'Oh God, if you are in such a situation after studying so much, what will happen to the likes of us?'

'Stop it yaar, Swapnil. Please let me study.'

But he didn't look up from his book. He was so engrossed in it that it looked like he was going through a porn magazine. Finally, we entered the classroom. I checked out which bench I had. I was wishing for the last or the second last bench. I saw my seat number on the bench. It was in the third row. Sameer got the first bench. My heartbeat increased. Swapnil had mini xerox notes in his pocket. He was not worried. I never had the courage to carry any xeroxes with me. We were sitting on our respective benches and waiting for the professor to enter the classroom. We all wanted a new teacher as the invigilator so that we could copy from each other easily. However, When I saw Deshmukh sir enter the classroom, I knew it was all over. Now no one could copy. He handed over the question paper to us along with the answer sheets. He warned us that if someone was caught cheating, he would be thrown out of the classroom.

I was going over the question paper. I knew four questions out of seven. I started solving the sums. I glanced at Swapnil. He had his xerox under his answer paper. He was writing at rocket speed. It made me more nervous. I glanced at Sameer. He was sitting idle, playing with his pen. That lessened my nervousness a bit. I glanced at Riya. She was writing sincerely. That motivated me to give my best in the paper as well. I attempted questions worth almost 70 marks, Riya 60 and Swapnil, Anup, and Sameer attempted questions almost worth 80 marks. We were satisfied with our performance based on whatever we had studied.

The second paper was also easy. Applied Science. The third paper was Computer Programming. I had studied for it well and had got my basics right. Everyone decided to come to my home and study for the night. Anup and Riya did not come. I did not want Riya to come home as my mom was already suspicious about her. Anup's parents did not allow him to go out at nights during exams. Sameer and Swapnil came home. We had dinner and started studying in my room.

We studied for a while. I taught them the basics of Programming. Since I had taught Programming to Riya before, she was done with this subject. Swapnil made a cup of tea for us.

'Hey Aadi, do you have a porn film?' Swapnil asked me.

'Are you crazy? We have exams in two days' time and you want to play with your dick? Shut up and study,' said Sameer.

He was a complete bookworm and was revising whatever I had taught him so far. At the end, Swapnil convinced me to show him a porn film. I had a small collection stacked in a secret drawer in my closet.

'Wow, she is so hot. Sameer look at her. What a shape she has!' Swapnil said pointing to one CD with a girl in a bikini on the cover.

'You go ahead and watch this while I go out and smoke.' Sameer had made his point.

'It helps your mind relax. After watching this, I can study with a refreshed mind,' Swapnil answered.

I also preferred to smoke over nude girls. It's not that we both were impotent or gay. But smoking gave us much more pleasure than watching porn. I believed we were at such an age that we should be doing it practically, not watching others do it. Swapnil said it was fun when no one was at home and you are studying late nights.

Tea, books, friends, porn films, cigarettes, and some studying in-between.

The next day, we sat for the Computer Programming exam. It was the worst paper I had ever given.

I looked at Swapnil's face. He gave me a smile. That made me more nervous. I looked at Sameer. He gave me a smile too for a change this time. It was like I was having a nervous breakdown. I looked at Anup. He was also writing. Heart failure. I looked at Riya. She was on her second page. I was dead. Three hours were spent looking at everyone's faces. I had attempted questions worth just 50 marks and was sure to fail.

'I screwed it up. I will fail. Sure kt,' I said to Riya after the exam.

'Jaan, don't worry. I know you will clear it,' assured Riya even though she seemed worried.

'Yes, maybe. Don't know. But I am sure of getting a KT.'

It was angry. I was the one who had taught everyone else what programming was and what computer language was. And today, I was standing outside the exam hall cursing myself.

My mind said, Welcome to engineering. Be ready for the worst.

The person who taught was about to fail and whoever he taught were about to pass.

I looked at Riya. She was talking to a few other friends and seemed least bothered. For the first time I felt like I was alone. I was hurt by her indifference towards me.

Making a Discovery

The exams had come to an end. I was worried about the Computer Programming results. The rest of the papers had gone fine though. All my friends, including Riya, decided to spend the next day chilling at my home.

'Bachcha, are you sure you want to come home? My mom will be there in the evening. I hope you will be comfortable in her company,' I asked Riya.

'Ya, it's totally fine. Plus I will leave early. May be before your mom comes home.'

'Hmm…ya, that would be fine. See you tomorrow then. Come along with Sameer. He knows the address.'

I was nervous as Riya was coming to my home for the first time. Sameer called me the next day.

'Hey Aadi…we are in front of your building. Shall we come upstairs?'

'Sure.'

No one was at home. I was alone. It was Anup and Riya.'s first visit to my home. The rest were already seated in my bedroom. We had rented a movie CD of *Kalyug*. We started watching it. Chips and popcorn was passed around in a bowl. Riya was sitting beside me with her head on my shoulder. We were teasing each other in between. I was playing with her lips and her eyes.

And then the song started—*jiya dhadak dhadak…* We both got lost in each other's eyes. Swapnil interrupted us by singing the same song. Riya punched Swapnil and told him to shut up.

'What's wrong with you, Swapnil?' Riya asked.

'Nothing, what did I say? I thought you both needed privacy. Let's go guys. You both enjoy yourselves in the bedroom.'

'Swapnil I will kill you.' Riya and Swapnil started running all over the house. I was watching them and their childlike behaviour. It looked like they were enjoying themselves. I was thankful to Swapnil for introducing me to Riya.

After lunch, we were relaxing when Riya showed all of them the ring that I had given her. She was showing it to each one of them personally with excitement. Swapnil hugged her, glad to see both of us happy. Everyone was happy for us.

They all decided to do something special for us. They made both of us stand face to face. Swapnil came and stood beside Riya, Anup and Sameer were beside me. Swapnil removed the ring from Riya's hand and gave it to me and he removed a gold ring from my hand and gave it to Riya.

'May I know what's happening?' I asked everyone.

Riya came close to me and gave a small peck on my lips and said, 'Jaan you are dumb. So please be quiet and just follow their instructions.'

Everbody laughed. I was still wondering what was happening around me.

Sameer started shooting with the camera.

'Sameer what is happening. Can anyone tell me please?'

'Your engagement. Now relax,' Swapnil shouted.

I was speechless. These were my friends for life. They were giving me something which I had always dreamt of.

I went close to Riya. They all started clapping and whistling.

I took Riya's hand in mine and put the ring on her finger. They applauded in joy. It was Riya's turn. She reciprocated the action by putting the ring on my finger. I could see happiness in her eyes. I could almost hear her heart beating. I could sense what she wanted to say.

'I love you a lot,' she said.

'Love you too.'

We went to our bedroom while the others watched the movie in the living room. I could feel the satisfaction in her eyes. I could sense her heartbeats saying we are engaged now. We will always be together. Some things cannot be said but felt. We didn't speak a word. But we still knew what we felt at that moment. We slept in each others' arms and looked at the ceiling. She kissed the ring on her finger and looked into my eyes. When she saw that I was almost on the verge of tears, she came closer and wiped off the tears from my eyes. We came outside in the living room. Everyone was engrossed in the movie.

Suddenly the doorbell rang. I saw the time. It was 6 pm. Time for mom to come back home.

'It's mom I think. Now what? We will be killed.'

'Now can't do anything. Go open the door,' Riya said.

I peeped through the keyhole and saw mom standing outside. I was afraid. Riya and mom were going to come face to face for the first time. Will they like each other? I could not go against either of them. At the same time, I could not live without either of them. I opened the door and there stood mom in front of all of us.

'My friends Swapnil, Sameer, Anup, and Riya are here. We are celebrating since exams are over,' I said in a nervous tone.

Mom came in and looked at each one of them. Especially Riya. Riya gave her a broad smile. I was so nervous. Mom did not speak a word and went straight into the kitchen. She made maggi noodles for all of us. After some time, mom called Riya in the kitchen.

'Riya, be nice. Don't argue and don't tell her about our relationship. Please,' I told her in a low voice as she went to the kitchen.

I could hear my mom saying something to Riya. I was trying to listen to their conversation.

'Aadi...just let her go. Riya wont do anything silly. Trust her,' said Sameer trying to reassure me.

'I trust Riya, but I also know how my mom is. She will ask her everything. I hope she doesn't go into panic mode.'

After about 30 minutes or so, Riya came back to the bedroom. I was looking at her and was just about to ask what had happened when she said, 'Aadi...your mom is so nice. You are lucky to have such a mom. She told me everything about you. I think she knows we are in a relationshp. I will be really happy to marry you and live at your home with your mom.'

'What? With my mom? You have to live with me. Not her,' I said jokingly.

'You won't understand a girl's feelings, Aadi. What it feels like to have a good mother-in-law and a good family after marriage. All these things mean a lot to me. When I leave my house and come to yours, you have to promise to take care of me.'

'Yes I will. Don't worry. Now let's have dinner and think of the upcoming exam results.'

'When will you grow up yaar? Riya has such sweet things to say about your future and you are telling her about the results. So unromantic,' Anup said.

'Dude, when the results are declared, all the romance will evaporate through your ass,' I replied. We all laughed and went to have dinner.

Everyone left soon after. I asked mom what she thought of my friends. She knew I was asking about Riya. Not 'everyone'. 'They are all nice. Riya too is sweet and innocent. She looks good with you. But concentrate on your studies for now. If you have a career, you can have a good life.' I was glad that my mom liked Riya. Our relationship had gone one more step ahead. Was everything happening too quickly?

❧❧

Finally the results were declared.

We called each other up and went to the college at around 7 pm. The results were put up on the notice board outside the library. There was such a big rush that we could not even see the board clearly. Riya was out with her parents and said she could not come. We decided to check the results again after some time. We went to the tapri outside. All of us were tensed.

'What do you think your result will be?' I asked both my friends.

Swapnil expected 1 KT and Anup expected 2. Sameer expected three. I was expecting one. It was a tough time for all of us. We were worried.

After a quick round of smoking, we went to the college. The crowd was much less than before. We went near the board and started searching for our names.

Swapnil was the first to see his name. One KT. As expected.

Sameer was the next to know that he had got 4 KTs. One more than expected. I was still looking for my name. Sameer's result made me nervous.

Next was Riya. Two KTs. This almost gave me a heart attack. She had got a KT in BEE and Mechanics.

Next was my turn. I had got 1 KT in CP.

Anup got 2 KTs.

Everyone had cleared Computer Programming. It made me feel low. Riya was not present at the scene. I so wanted to tell her about the results. But she was spending time with her family. She had got 2 KTs. I wondered how her family would react to it. I did not want to tell her the results over the phone and spoil her day. I called my mom. She was not happy. But she did not say anything. One KT was fine when a few months earlier I never even wanted to do engineering. Mom asked me about Riya's result. I did not say anything and kept the phone down.

I called Riya a few hours later. She was with her family. I did not tell her about the results.

I messaged her later.

Results are out. I have got 1 KT. Sameer four. Swapnil one. Anup two. And you two as well. In BEE and Mechanics.

There was no reply. I was worried. Was she upset? I messaged her again.

```
What happened? Is everything okay? Did you tell
your parents about your result?
```

This time also there was no reply. I was tensed. I called her up but she did not pick up the phone. That made me more tensed.

I went back home and retired to bed soon after. When I got up in the morning, I saw there was a message from her.

```
Sorry, I was busy with my family so could not
reply sooner. I hope you're not angry with me.
Sorry again. Anyway congrats for the result.
Call me when you get up.
```

I immediately called her up. She picked up the phone on the first ring.

'What the hell is this? Where were you all day yesterday? I called you atleast 20 times and left you so many messages. Were you really with your parents? Or were you out with someone on a date?'

'Aadi...why are you being so rude? You know I was with my family. I had told you that. They were around me all the time. How could I have talked to you in front of them?'

'I don't care. You should have. Get lost. I do not want to talk to you. I hate you.'

'Fine. Do as you feel like. You are extremely rude. Hate you too. Bye.'

I was really disturbed by the result and Riya was behaving very badly. I knew I should not have shouted at her but I had lost my temper. For the first time we had fought like this. I felt bad. However, it was her mistake this time and I wanted her to realize it. I did not call back.

Let her go to hell, I thought. I had called her non-stop for almost 10 hours. I had even left her so many messages. Not getting a reply from her was too much for me to bear.

I did not talk with Riya for one whole day. I was disturbed about my result. I had got 29 marks in CP. Somehow I wanted to clear the paper. I had heard that there were a few professors who would charge around 10,000 rupees and get the paper cleared in revaluation. I was ready to do that. Swapnil and I went to meet a few of those professors. Finally we were able to track down one of them. But he was asking for 20,000 rupees. It was not a small amount for us. Though he told us to give the paper for revaluation, he did not look trustworthy. I desperately wanted to clear the paper in any possible way. I had tried everything. If Riya had been with me, my confidence would have soared. But I was alone.

Realizing that she was not going to call me, I took the initiative and called her instead. As soon as she picked up the phone, she started crying. It hurt me to see her cry and made me realize I was wrong. I aplogized to her. She cried even more.

'Jaan, I am sorry. Please say something. Stop crying, bachcha. Please forgive me.'

'Why didn't you call me for so long? I was waiting for your call from the time I kept the phone down. You don't care about me. You have started taking me for granted. Why Aadi…why? I had told you everything that day. I needed you the most when my parents shouted at me for the exam results. But you were not there. I hate you Aadi…' she cried.

'I said sorry, baba. Let's go to Bandra tomorrow. Mount Mary.'

'Okay fine. Dare you fight with me again. Please. I can't handle this. Love you. And sorry once again.'

'Don't be sorry. It was my mistake and I will not repeat it, I promise. See you tomorrow.'

We met the next day. She was still upset for whatever had happened. I knew how to make her happy. I had a surprise for her.

'Are you still angry with me?' I asked her after taking a rickshaw from Bandra.

'Ya, somewhat,' she replied looking at me with swollen eyes. I cursed myself for having made her cry so much.

'I know how to make you smile, don't I?' I said kissing her forehead.

'What? Don't tell me you have a surprise for me?' she said with a quizzical impression.

'Hmm…kind of.' I opened the zip of my bag, took out the wrapped gift, and gave it to her. She kissed me so hard that it left a big love bite on my neck. She started unwrapping her present.

It was a T-shirt with a smiley at the centre and the word 'Sorry' written right below it. She hugged me as tightly as she could.

It is such a wonderful feeling when your love kisses you and hugs you after a fight. We had not talked to each other for almost two days. But here we were after two days, kissing and hugging each other, crying in each other's arms as if nothing had happened. We both knew that we could not live without each other.

I told her about the revaluation and that I had had a talk with a professor who would clear my paper. Oh God! I wanted to say 'our' paper but had said 'my' paper by mistake. She did not take this very well.

'Good. Very good. You did not feel like telling me this in the past two days and here you are accusing me of not having called you. You took such a big decision without even asking me. I understand we are not talking to each other but did you forget that even I had a KT? You could have told him to re-evaluate my paper too. You have changed Aadi…'

'I didn't mean it. Why would I tell him just about myself? I have not decided if I will go for re-evaluation or not. Why are you overreacting? For God's sake, please stop fighting.'

A long silence followed.

She suddenly burst into a big smile. She did not want to waste time in fighting. I went and kissed her. All the tension between us evaporated in a second. We went to Mount Mary. Bandstand—kissing, hugging, fondling each other, looking at the waves of the sea. But in my heart I knew our relationship would never be the same. Little cracks had begun to appear. Small fights today, bigger ones tomorrow. I didn't know where our relationship was headed.

A New Semester

It was the end of our vacations and the beginning of the second semester. Going back to college was not an exciting thought at all. Riya had reached college before me. I told her to collect the marksheets for both of us. When I reached college, I met Riya in the quadrangle. We both went to the notice board to note down the subjects and timetable.

1. CP 2
2. ENGG DRAWING
3. APPLIED SCIENCES 2
4. MATHS 2
5. COMMUNICATION SKILLS

The subjects were not as difficult as the ones we had in the first semester. Of course Maths 2 and CP 2 were a bit tricky. However, the rest of the subjects were manageable. We went for our first lecture of the second semester. I gave Riya a missed call in the middle of the lecture and she looked back and gave me a naughty smile. We fought often, but still loved each other from the bottom of our hearts. It was barely the first day of the second semester, and love was in the air.

We were having lunch in our classroom when I went out to attend a call. I was approached by two boys when I was on call.

'Do you know that girl?' both asked me in unison.

'Who are you talking about?' I asked. They pointed to a girl in the class and I peeped in to look. It was Riya! They were asking me her name. I tried to avoid the question. I gave them a different name.

'No, don't try to fool us. That's not her name, we know. Her name is something else,' they said. However, I did not reveal her name to them. Judging that I was not going to reveal her name, come what may, they left soon after. I went into the classroom and sat next to Riya. Swapnil and my other friends were sitting on the last bench. I was talking to Riya when I again saw the two boys standing outside the back door. They were gesturing for me to come out. I chose to ignore them and continued talking to Riya. She was telling me about her brother's upcoming exams.

Suddenly they entered the classroom and came and stood near us. I wanted to keep Riya away from them. I thought they were going to ask her for her name or something else. But nothing like that happened.

They came closer to me and said, 'What's your problem?' Before I could reply, they slapped me hard and ran away. I was shocked. All this had happened in a fraction of a second. Everyone in the class was looking at me. Sameer and Swapnil came running towards me. They were equally shocked. Riya just kept staring at me. She did not know what exactly had happened. Who were they and why did they hit me?

Sameer came rushing towards me and asked, 'What happened, Aadi? Who were they? Did you say anything?'

'I really don't know. They had approached me when I went outside to attend a call. They asked me about Riya and left. I ignored them at that time. This time they came and before I could say anything, they just slapped me. I would have grabbed them and hit them hard if I had the chance. But it all happened so quickly that I had no time to react.'

'What the fuck! How can someone just come and hit you like this? Let me look into the matter,' Sameer said.

'Even I don't know. I don't even know their names,' I said. I was getting increasingly frustrated.

We went out of the classroom to search for them. But we could not find them anywhere. We came into the classroom and attended the lecture. Everyone was disturbed. Riya was looking at me throughout the lecture. She was more disturbed than I was, especially after knowing that they had hit me because of her. She had that guilty look in her eyes. I messaged her and asked her to concentrate on the lecture and not worry about anything.

Sameer and I decided to find out more about the two guys and take appropriate action. The next day we came to know that the person who had hit me was Rishi. He was the son of some local minister. Minister or a peon's son, we did not care. We had arranged for a group of boys to hit him back. Riya was unaware of our plan. I wanted to keep her away from all of this. I did not want her to get into any sort of trouble. We waited outside the college gate patiently. After some time, we saw him coming. Since he knew me by face, I went and stood away from the group. Sameer called him and asked him what had happened the previous day in college. He did not say anything about me. I went near them. He saw me and remembered.

'You bastard! You thought you could hit me and run away so easily, didn't you? I don't care who you are. I dare you to look at Riya again. If you even ask about her, I will kill you.'

Sameer came forward and slapped him. He also counter-attacked us. But we were in a group and he was alone. We clearly outnumbered him. We hit him badly. He fell down on the road. We were still hitting him when Sameer stopped us. As he got up, I slapped him hard and said, 'Last warning.'

He said sorry immediately and admitted that he was not any minister's son. He was just showing off in front of the first-year students. He also promised never to look at Riya again.

We left the scene. I did not utter a word about this to Riya. When she enquired about my whereabouts, I told her that my phone was on silent and apologized for not taking her calls.

Riya was still worried about the incident. I consoled her and told her that everything was normal and that he wouldn't trouble us again. She smiled and we went for our practicals.

❧❧

The annual college function was about to begin in two days. We were all very excited. I was happy as there were going to be no lectures during that time. Riya and I decided to attend college only on the days when there were some traditional functions or when it was a sari day. For the rest of the time, we decided we would spend some time together hanging out somewhere.

Then came Black Day, a day when we were all supposed to wear black coloured clothes to college. I told Riya that black did not suit her complexion and asked her to wear something different. I wanted my jaan to look the best. She said she would shock me by her outfit. I was eagerly waiting for her near the college gate. As she approached me, I was stunned.

She was wearing a gorgeous dress. It was short, barely covering her bottom. She was looking like an absolute beauty. We went into the college and met everyone. From there, we went to a nearby restaurant and ate paav bhaaji as usual.

Each day had something new to offer. The sari day came next. It was tied up with the Miss Fresher competition. The girl who got the maximum roses would be crowned Miss Fresher. Riya was looking absolutely gorgeous in her blue sari. And her blouse was backless. We did not wait in college. I wanted to spend time alone with her. We went to Grant Lane, Vashi.

'You are looking so good. I can't believe I have the pleasure of having you in my life,' I said.

'You're looking no less sexy in your sherwaani. Love you too,' she said.

We spent some time in Grant Lane and came back to college. When I reached college, I saw that Sameer was giving a rose to some girl but she rejected his proposal. He tried hard to convince her. I felt sad for him.

Then came the Annual Day—the day for which we had waited for a long time. it was the last day of celebrations. We had a fashion show and a DJ night too. There was a competition of eating the maximum chillies on stage. Everyone was forcing me to participate in the competition and I finally gave in to their request.

There was another boy in the competition against me. The anchor made his customary announcement, 'The two of you have to eat as many chillies as possible in 1 minute. The one who eats the maximum number of chilles in 1 minute will get 1000 rupees. Your time starts now.'

I started eating. Three chillies down, my mouth was burning. Another chilly and it was on fire. What the fuck! I wanted to quit right there and then. I wanted to urgently use the washroom. I could not handle the pressure. The match was over. I lost. There was no chance for me to win.

' Please let me go to the washroom,' I requested soon after the competition was over.

My mouth was burning. I drank a full bottle of water and went to the washroom.

'You idiots. I am screwed. Give me more water,' I said to everyone.

' Drink, my bachcha. I can feel what you are going through. I am loving it.' Riya was laughing at my condition.

Even though I was suffering, I had atleast succeeded in making them laugh. We had enjoyed ourselves very much the day. Riya was with me. My friends were with me. We had had lots of fun. I felt like I was complete. I had good friends to fall back on, my love, and the college life I always wanted.

Meeting Riya's Friends

Neha and Riya had been close friends since school days. Neha had been in the same school as Riya and they were now in the same college. Since they were in different sections, they did not get an apportunity to interact much during college hours. Neha had shifted to Hyderabad for two years and was now back in Mumbai for higher studies.

Once when Riya and I were standing near the bus depot, we saw her walking towards us. Riya called out to her and introduced us.

'Hi Neha. How have you been? This is Aditya. We are from same division. Actually…we are dating and love each other very much.'

'Hi, Aditya. Beware of her. Don't regret your decision to be with her later,' she said light-heartedly.

'Don't worry, I won't regret ever. And the day I will regret it, I will call you and tell you that you were right.'

Riya gave me an angry look. 1 apologized. We all laughed.

'What is up with you? What about your relationship with Amit?' Riya asked her.

'Oh, you still remember him. Great. I thought you must have erased his name from your memory.'

'Are you crazy. How can I? He used to love you so much. How is he now? Does he look the same? I haven't seen him since the last 3 years.'

'Lucky you. I am waiting for him. He is coming in 5 minutes.'

From their conversation, I came to know that he also lived in the same locality as Riya and Neha. He fell in love with Neha during school days though their relationship began after school, but as Neha moved to Hyderabad, they lost touch. Now they were both together. True love, I thought. After living separately for 2 years, they were still together. I admired them and their relationship.

'There he is,' said Neha pointing at him. He was too far. We could not see him clearly. As he came closer, I observed him carefully.

He was tall. Taller than me. Maybe 5 feet 10 inches. Dark complexioned. Muscled body. A very odd shirt though. Pink in colour. I thought he looked gay. He was wearing black aviators and Nike shoes.His low waist jeans were ripped at the bottom.

'This is Amit. My Amit,' said Neha grabbing his waist and leaning on him.

On seeing Riya he said excitedly, 'Riya is this really

you? I cannot believe this. Oh my God. Where were you for so many years? I am seeing you after such a long time.'

What does he mean by 'where were you for so many years'? I thought angrily to myself. She is mine, you gay. Only mine.

Riya replied, 'My goodness. You have changed a lot since the last time I saw you. Really. Back then you were so thin. You have put on weight now. Nice muscles.'

I looked at my muscles. I felt insecure as I did not have any. Do muscles mean everything? Why does any one need muscles in the first place? If you are smart looking, intelligent, and have power in your rod, why should you need muscles? Moreover, if you can understand what your girl wants from you, why need muscles?

'Meet him. This is Aadi...my jaan. My everything. I love him beyond words can describe,' said Riya finally introducing me.

I said an awkward hi to him. His reaction was no different. It was the same as mine. Maybe he was thinking why Riya had chosen me. I wanted to tell him because I was not gay like him and would never wear a pink T-shirt. However, I kept mum.

What was happening to me? Why was I getting so insecure? I told myself to calm down. Riya was mine. Maybe I was feeling so because she had appreciated a man in front of me for the first time. But somewhere at the back of my mind, I knew I was her one and only jaan. That made me feel much better.

'Where are the two of you going? We are going to have something in the restaurant. Do you want to join us?' Riya asked them.

I looked at Riya in anger. Why do you want the two of them? Let them go their way. We will go our way. I wanted privacy. I did not want to indulge in stupid conversations with the both of them. I was the stranger here since all of them knew each other from before.

Neha and Amit agreed.

Superb! Excellent! Bloody idiots! Don't you understand Riya asked you just for formality? Who is going to foot the bill? I will not pay a single penny. Let Amit pay it. He wanted to join us, right? What the hell? Riya looked at me. She knew what I was thinking. She gave me a sweet smile. I knew she did not want them to come but had to do it out of courtesy. However, fools will be fools. Who can change them?

We ordered some snacks.

'Amit doesn't have oily food. He is health conscious,' Neha added.

Oh really, so what can we do? Keep your Amit in your showcase as a showpiece. A HEALTH CONSCIOUS MAN.

I called the waiter on purpose and placed my order. 'Bring me paav bhaaji,' I said to him.

'Anything more, sir?' he asked.

'Yes, put some more oil. I like oily food.' They all stared at me. Riya pinched my thigh under the table. I looked at her and gave her a broad smile. She knew what I was trying to do.

They were chatting about school days. I was sitting quietly watching them talk about old stuff from school about which I had no clue. What was I supposed to say? Again, Neha started with 'my Amit' stuff.

'We have to leave early. Its time for my Amit's gym,' she said playing with his short hair.

I was irritated. I was losing control. Riya gestured with her eys for me to calm down. My Amit, my Amit, my Amit! I thought he was her pussycat or some pet. How she went on and on about him was disgusting.

We left after some time.

'Jaan, I hate this. Why did they have to join us? You know I don't like all this,' I said angrily.

She answered me with a kiss in the middle of the road. It was a small kiss, but it was enough to calm me down.

A Day of Surprises

February 26. Riya and I had decided to spend the entire day together. It was my first birthday with her. We had decided to go to Grant Lane. We met each other at 11 am at Aerol Depot. We went there by bus. She had two surprises for me. I was excited. I wanted this day to be special.

As the bus left Aerol, she gave me a white rose. I was really touched by her thoughtfulness.

'Why white rose jaan?' I asked her.

'We have been fighting so much these past few days. So I wanted to give you a white rose to say that I really don't want us fighting in future.'

'You are a sweetheart.' I was really touched by her first gift. It was such a special way to express her love.

After a few minutes, she took out something from her bag. I watched her carefully. She was looking at me and smiling.

'Now what? How many gifts have you brought along?' I was excited.

'Bachcha, have patience. Close your eyes,' she said putting her hand over my eyes.

She placed something in my hand and asked me to open my eyes. I lifted the lid to see that there was a dark pink rose this time. This was so touching. She was really making my day more beautiful with each passing second.

'What is this for?' I did not know the significance of a dark pink rose.

'This is to thank you. Thank you for whatever you have done for me so far and for being with me.'

'Thanks.' She had again left me speechless. I kissed her on the cheeks.

We reached Grant Lane. As we sat in the auto, she again put her hands in the bag. Now what? Is this a dream?

'Hey, you said you had just two gifts. Now what is it?'

She pulled out a lavender colour rose from her bag. It was my third rose of the day in the last 40 minutes. Why did she love me so much?

'Jaan what has happened to you? When did you plan all this?'

'You just enjoy your birthday. I will keep making it more special.'

'You have already made it special, jaan.'

'What does this colour mean?'

'This means love at first sight. I loved you from the day I first saw you. From the day our eyes met, when I entered the classroom. I started loving you from that day onwards. I wanted you to be mine from that moment itself. Love you so much.'

We got down from the auto and there she was again in front of me with a yellow rose. I wanted to cry now. I just could not believe my eyes.

We hugged each other so tightly that alll the passersby looked at us. We did not care. This time I knew the meaning of the yellow rose. It meant she cared for me. She did care for me. A lot.

We entered the garden and sat on a bench. I was just looking into her eyes. I wanted to forget every fight I had had with her. I wanted to forget all those times I had doubted her. I kissed her. For the first time while kissing her, I closed my eyes. As I opened my eyes, I saw a red rose kept on my bag which was kept beside me.

She handed over the rose to me and said:

'I love you a lot. I love you more than anything in the world. There may be many girls who will love you in future. But trust me, you will never get a girl like me who will do all these things for you. And I am not doing these things to show you that I am the best but I am doing this because you are the best. You are the best possible thing that could have ever happened in my life. My love for you is increasing day by day. Let's get married.'

After a pause she said, 'I know we can't. However, I want to be with you for 24 hours atleast. From the time you wake up until the time you sleep.'

I grabbed her and gave her a tight squeeze. I couldn't control myself and bit her on her lips. She cried in ecstasy. She was mine…just mine. No one could have her in their life now.

We were both lost in our world. I went to order some food from a nearby dhaba. I ordered veg chilly and told the man to bring it to the garden. As I walked towards the bench, I saw that she had kept a cake on the bench with a candle on it. On it was written '*To my sweet cute bachhu.*'

This time I could not stop my tears. She stood up and came close to me. She gave me the warmest hug. Each moment was special. I blew out the candle and cut my birthday cake. I forced the first piece into her mouth. She was unable to speak. She did the same with me. It was a small cake and both of us gobbled it up. After eating the cake and veg chilly, I slept with my head on her lap. I was looking into her eyes and she was weeping. I could not stop my tears as well.

We relaxed ourselves on the bench in each other's arms. I saw the time. It was 4 pm. We had slept for almost 2 hours. Her head was on my chest. I did not get up. I wanted to see her sleeping. On the previous occasion, she had not woken me up. It was my turn now. She finally woke up after 15 minutes.

'Jaan, it's half past four. We have slept for almost 2 hours. Thank god our belongings are safe.'

'Oh my God. What are you saying? But don't worry…we still have a few hours left to ourselves. Let me show you something.'

One more rose? I would have fallen down on the grass. So many gifts. So many surprises.

'Bachcha enough. I am already full of gifts. Why do you love me so much?'

'Because you are special.' She took out a plastic bag from her purse.

It was a green T-shirt from Pepe Jeans. I knew it was expensive. From where did she get so much money?

This time I hade no words to explain what I felt.

Now it was my turn. It was my turn to give her something. She had done so much for me. Now I would return the favour. Even I had a few things in mind for her that evening.

We left Grant Lane at about 5 pm and went to Neel restaurant. I had searched for that restaurant earlier on the Internet. I had informed the manager about all the arrangements.

We reached the destination. I told her to wait. I went inside and confirmed with the manager if everything was ready.

I called Riya inside. It had a long, dark passage. There were two tables in the hall that gave complete privacy to couples. It was surrounded by ply from three sides and it had a round table at the centre with two chairs. It also had a fancy candle placed at the centre and rose petals sprinkled on top of it. There were a few other people dining in the restaurant.

However, we had our own space since I had booked one of the two tables that gave full privacy to us. I had asked them to arrange for a candlelight dinner.

This time there were tears in her eyes. She pinched my hand so hard that it hurt me. She wanted to kiss me but could not because the waiter was coming to take the order. I told the waiter to play our special song.

Tujhe dekh dekh sona…

As the song started, she could not stop herself from kissing me.

'Did you like my surprise? I know this is nothing compared to what you did for me today,' I said

'No sweetheart, you are the best. If I combine all the gifts that I gave you, they were nothing in front of what you did for me right now.'

My surprises were not over yet. One surprise remained. We left the restaurant after a nice dinner and reached Grant Lane station. This was something which could backfire and go against me. However, I was willing to take the risk.

When the train reached Aerol, Riya was about to get down but I stopped her. She told me she was getting late. Still I told her to come with me. We reached my area and then my apartment. Mom opened the door. She was surprised to see together. Mom was alone at home. We sat in the hall. Mom brought us two glasses of water.

I said, 'Mom I love Riya. I love her very much. We love each other very much.'

My mom was shocked. She hadn't seen this coming. Riya's jaw dropped as she was stunned with the last surprise of the day.

A Nervous Meeting

More than 30 minutes had passed and there was still silence in the room. I was sitting on the sofa. Mom and Riya were sitting on a couch. Mom first looked at me and then at Riya. I was trying to read her mind. Finally, I broke the silence.

'Mom say something. Please. I really love her.'

My mom had always been frank with me. We were more like friends than mother and son and I shared almost everything that mattered to me with her. I wanted her to support me. I wanted her to accept Riya as my girlfriend.

'Is this your age to get married? Do you even know what love is? Bunking colleges and roaming around hand in hand, watching movies…do you think this is love?'

'Mom I don't know what it is. But the one thing I do know is that I like her. I want her to be with me.'

'Do whatever you want. What can I say?' she said looking visibly upset.

Riya directed me to go inside. I went without saying anything. Maybe in my absence mom would talk to

Riya frankly about me. Or it could be the other way round too.

I left my bedroom door ajar and was listening to their conversation. 'When did all this start? What exactly happened? And how far have you gone in your relationship?' mom asked Riya.

'Aunty, I know I may be wrong. You have seen more of life than us kids. Nevertheless, we seriously like each other. I don't know when or how it happened, but it did. And we have been in a relationship since November. He helped me in my studies or whenever I was in trouble. He is very nice to me. I do not know if this is love or not. But ...'

'So you've been together since November? I knew something was brewing between you two ever since Aditya started coming late to home. But I never confronted him about it as I wanted him to concentrate on his exams. What are you both up to? First learn to earn money and stand on your own feet, then indulge in all these things.'

'Aunty, I know this is not the right age for all this. But if you try to separate both of us, it would affect our semester. Aunty, do not worry, I will take care of him. Seriously, I will not let him deviate from studies. Please trust me.'

I saw mom's face break into a smile and I was relieved. I wanted to hug her. She had accepted Riya after all.

I went outside for I could not hide my happiness.

'So you heard everything, didn't you? I am your mom. So don't act smart with me,' she chided.

She told me that education should always be my first priority and all the rest could come later. I accepted all her terms and conditions. After all, she had accepted my Riya.

Riya was very happy. We chatted for sometime and then I dropped her home.

♧♧

Our relationship had moved one more step ahead.

I dreamt of getting engaged to her. A hall filled with family and friends. When she would ask me what kind of a wedding I wished for, I would answer, 'Nothing special. Just one that makes me your husband legally at the end of the day.'

'Mom, do you really like Riya?' I asked her when I reached back home. I wanted to know the truth.

'Yes I like her. I think she is the only girl who can reform you. However, as I said before, studies are the first priority.'

I had got the best gift from my parents on my birthday. Riya. My Jaan.

Special Moments

I reached college by 10 am the next day. Riya had messaged me in the morning saying that she would be late due to some household work. The second lecture had begun. Riya was still at home. She messaged me to come to her home. I was surprised. I knew there was no one else at her house. When the lecture got over, I left college and reached her gate.

'Hey, shall I come inside? What if the watchman asks me for my identity card or something'? I asked her over the phone.

'He won't say anything. Just come inside,' she said and hung up.

I went inside and rang the doorbell. She came running and opened the door. I entered her house and saw Amit and Neha already seated there. Not again, I said to myself. They were having chips. Now wasn't that oily? Fools will be fools. I went straight into the kitchen and Riya joined me.

'What is this? What are these two doing here?'

'They are here to celebrate your birthday. I had called Neha in the morning and told her what had happened yesterday. So she said she would get Amit along so we could all celebrate your birthday together.'

'That's ridiculous. It was my birthday. Why did these two want to celebrate it? And if they wanted to celebrate, who the hell was giving them a party?'

'Please Aadi… they are nice. Let's go outside,' Riya said pulling my shirt's collar.

They wished me belated happy birthday. They looked nice together as a couple. But I was insecure in their company. I felt left out.

Riya was in the kitchen preparing something to eat. Neha also went inside and this made me even more irritated. I was alone sitting with Amit. We were watching TV. I did not talk to him. He did not try talking to me either. We did not even look at each other. He was kind of reserved and so was I. Moreover, I hated him. I wanted to be alone at my girlfriend's house and there he was, sitting in front of me in her house like she was his girl friend.

He asked me for water. I looked at him but did not oblige. I wanted to tell him that this was 'my' Riya's house. I could do anything I wanted.

Riya and Neha came out as they were almost ready with the food.

'I hope you are having a nice time together,' Riya said.

Ya right! Nice time with a gay, I said to myself. The biggest irritant was that he carried an N-series Nokia cell phone that was all the rage then. But he had it in pink colour. Urgh!

Riya came and sat beside me. and Neha were discussing something which we could not hear. I did not care to.

'So how is your love life?' Amit asked Riya with a big smile on his face. I hated that smile.

'Can't you see, we are madly in love with each other. We cannot live without each other. I love him a lot.' Her answer brought a big smile on my face.

'What about you?' I asked Neha. I wanted to show Amit that if he could talk to my girlfriend, so could I.

'Even we love each other. It has been a difficult journey for us. Still we are together. This gives us great satisfaction,' Neha answered.

'Ya even I love her a lot,' Amit added.

For the first time I was not angry at his answer. Not even frustrated. I was observing their eyes. Maybe they did love each other like they said.

We decided to play cards. Teen patti.

I shuffled the cards and gave three cards to each. I looked at my cards.

I had three cards of spades.

We put in a minimum bet of 10 rupees. For the first round, nobody packed their cards. The second round began. Riya packed and so did Neha. Now only Amit and I were left.

'I increase the bet by 20 rupees,' I said.

'Me too,' Amit added.

'I will further increase it by 20 rupees. Amit think it over. You will lose,' I warned him.

'Don't worry. I call for a show,' he replied cheekily.

'I showed him my cards one by one.

'I told you that you will lose. Didn't I? See your face.'

He showed me the first card. It was the queen of hearts. I looked at my queen of hearts. I wished I had that card. I could have afforded to lose but for that card. He showed me the second card. It was the queen of spade. Two queens. This made me nervous. It was not the question of a few rupees but the question of who was superior between the two of us.

He showed me the third card now. It was a joker. I had lost.

'Buddy, one should never be overconfident. This is how a real game ought to be played. You have to win without saying a word,' he said getting up with a look of pride on his face, like he had won a battle or something.

I hated him so much. I wanted to win. I kept telling myself it was just a game. However, I did not forget what he had said.

It was time to have lunch. Both the girls went inside to warm up the food, leaving Amit and me behind. This time I took the initiative and talked to him first.

'So, how is college going on?'

'Perfect. What about you?'

'Nothing special. So you love Neha or are you dating her just for sex?' I thought he would hit me.

He laughed and said, 'Ya I really love her. We've been together for a long time now.'

I had got my answer. I had known there was something off about him from the day I first saw him.

'Your parents know about it?' I was eager to hear his response.

'Not yet. But let's see. Our parents are strict. Neha's dad will kill her if he gets to know about our relationship. They don't believe in love and all.'

I had seen parents like theirs before. Not everybody was as lucky to get parents like mine. I was observing him carefully. There was something going on in his mind. One thing was sure. This man couldn't love anyone. If someone had asked me that question, I would not have spared him.

Riya came out with the food. Neha followed her with the dishes. I was waiting to taste it as I was going to have fish made by Riya for the very first time.

Riya served all of us and came and sat beside me. I was looking at her. She gave a smile. She understood why I was looking at her. She played with my hair a little.

Soon we started eating. The food was delicious. Riya started feeding me and I did the same.

'Like it?' She knew I loved her cooking but for some strange reason she would always ask.

'Of course I like it. You are a great cook.'

She was changing the TV channels when Pogo appeared and I told her to stop.

'Are you a kid? My brother watches these cartoons,' Riya laughed.

'Don't you call me bachcha? Then I am a kid. I love this show. I love *Bob the Builder*,' I smiled like a kid.

'Idiot. Wait I will bring rice for you,' she said and went into the kitchen.

'Hey Aadi… Why do you like this show?' Amit asked me.

I chose to ignore him and quickly changed the topic. Riya served me rice and fed me with a spoon. I loved watching her eyes when she fed me. I would end up eating more rice because of this.

Riya fulfilled all my needs and guided me to the right path, wiped away my tears, and tried to make me feel happy when I was low and depressed. I always felt like telling her that I loved her much more than I had ever before.

After having lunch, we went to the bedroom. I wanted to talk to Riya. I wanted to spend some quality time with her. Amit and Neha were in the hall. We closed the door of the bedroom and sat on the bed.

'Jaan, you are a very nice cook. I loved all the dishes.' She kept her head on my lap and lay on the bed.

'Thanks. I feared that you would not like it. Now I can marry you in peace.'

'Marry me? So early?' I asked.

'Yes. I want to.' She was serious.

But I felt it was too early to get married.

She started showing me her old photographs and some soft toys. Her dresses and her skirts. I loved one mini skirt in particular. It was grey in colour and shorter than all the skirts I had seen her wear before. I told her to wear that one. She refused as the other two were sitting outside.

'Change here. I will close my eyes. I won't see you changing,' I said.

'Dare you open your eyes,' she said.

'I won't open my eyes but I will open your skirt for sure,' I said flirtatiously. I was best at doing that. Atleast I thought so.

'Shut up, Aadi. Now open your eyes,' she said.

I was gazing at her so hard that I fell down from the bed. My heart skipped a beat. She had changed her top too. It was her new red top. Red was my weakness. Seeing that colour, I could not resist myself. I pushed her onto the bed.

As we lay facing each other, listening to Mariah Carey, I looked into her eyes, leaned over, and said, 'You are awesome.'

She was playing with my bare chest. This was the first time we were together in bed. The first time I got naked with Riya.

Her voice was steady and soft, her lips close to my ear. At the same moment, my hands were securely wrapped around her back and my chest was pressed against hers. Later, as we lay facing each other, listening to John Mayer's 'Your body is a wonderland', she looked into my eyes, leaned in, and said, 'You're amazing in bed.'

'You want me to try it in the air?' I said becoming more naughty.

'You make me feel so good,' she sighed.

'The next time I am going to take you on a horseride,' I said hugging her as we lay beside each other.

She looked fresh after making love. Her face glittered. We went outside after sometime. Neha and Amit were watching TV.

All three of us left the house shortly afterwards. I was tired and did not want to travel by train. I decided to go by autorickshaw. I was still engrossed in Riya's perfume, her body, her expressions—all of it haunted me. After physically, mentally, and emotionally becoming a single living and breathing soul, I did not want to let go of her.

I was about to reach home when Riya called me. I picked up the phone.

'So you're missing me so much that I get a call barely 20 minutes after I've left your house? Love you jaan,' I said as I picked up the call.

'Jaan, listen to me first. Please. It's urgent. Please come back'

'What happened? Something serious? Are you okay?' I said in a tense voice.

'Yes, its serious. Amit has met with an accident. He fell from his bike. He had dropped Neha home and while he was on his way back home, his bike skid on the highway. Neha just called me to tell me this. Please come back. We are taking him to the hospital. We are on our way to the hospital. Sector 20.'

'Okay fine. Don't worry. I am coming.' I hated him, but for Riya and Neha's sake, I had to go.

I told the driver to stop. I paid him, got down, and went to Aerol again. I reached the hospital. Riya and Neha were standing at the reception. Neha was crying. I tried to console her. The doctor told us that it was nothing serious. He had a minor fracture in his hand. I went inside to see him.

'Aadi, how come you are here?' He was surprised seeing me in hospital. Maybe he knew that I hated him all along.

'Riya called me up. I came to see if anything was serious. However, you seem to be fine. Just a minor crack. Right?' I had a look at his hand.

'Ya kind of. Maybe 20 days to recover. I was driving slowly but…'

'Its okay. Take rest. And be careful. Shall I leave? I will come back again tomorrow. I am late now. I have to reach home.'

Riya was waiting outside. I calmed her down. She was worried. I told them to go home as it was getting late. All of us left the hospital. I dropped them first and then went back home.

I was already late. I told mom what had happened. I just said that my friend had met with an accident. My 'college' friend. If I had told her everything, she would have asked more questions.

The next morning I went to the hospital to check upon Amit. His didi was already there with him. I asked him how he was feeling. He smiled.

'When are you getting discharged?' I asked him.

'Maybe tomorrow. The doctor will examine me today and then he will take the decision. I hope he discharges me today. There are no sexy nurses here.' We all laughed.

Amit's didi told me to wait with him for a little while since she had to rush back home urgently for some work.

'Aadi you are very lucky.' He seemed upset.

'Why. Any problem? What's the matter?'

'You have such a nice girlfriend who takes care of you. You are a lucky boy,' he added.

When I asked him the details, he started telling me about his love life.

Neha has not called me since last night. It is already 11 am. Is this the way to behave? She doesn't care about how I feel or what I want. She could have waited here with me yesterday. However, she said she was sleepy and left. It's not the case with you and Riya. I am sure if something like this had happened to you, the case would have been completely different. I seriously love Neha but she does not return my love. I understand her family is strict but still these things can be worked out. The way she gets close to other boys irritates me. Whenever I call her during lunchtime, she says she is busy with her other friends. I wait outside your college for hours and she still does not bunk a lecture. Here I am, still with her, as I truly love her.

I thought about how right he was. Riya truly was a sweetheart. She would have taken a bed next to me just to be with me in the hospital. However, as I said before, not everybody could have Riya. She was mine and just mine.

'Look Amit, do you seriously love her? Frankly telling you, I have been observing Neha and you since the first day I met you. I think you are not at all serious about her. Instead, you just want her to go to bed with you. I do not know how far and how deep your relationship is but I think she is a good girl. Don't compare her with anyone. If you love her, don't expect anything. Just go on loving her.'

'Aadi... I am not with her for sex. I could get that for money anywhere else. I want her love. I do not say she doesn't love me. However, she has different priorities. Such things hurt me.'

Somewhere in my heart, I felt that he really loved Neha. I told myself that I ought to give him a chance. But I could not believe Neha was at fault. She seemed like a nice girl to me. Anyways, there was no point in thinking so much. I decided to give Amit one more chance.

'Friends?' I moved a hand of friendship towards him.

'I considered you as a friend much earlier,' he replied.

We looked at each other and smiled. Neha entered the room. It was 12 pm. I said goodbye to both of them and left. Riya was in college. I messaged her that I was coming. On the way to college, I thought if that was a handshake of true friendship or did he have some other plans in mind?

The Seven Promises

Amit was discharged on Thursday. He was allowed to go to college from the next day onwards. He still had a bandage on his right hand. But it was nothing serious. The four of us decided to go to Chowpatty on Saturday. I asked Swapnil, Sameer, and Anup if they were coming. Sameer had some work and couldn't come. Swapnil and Anup happily tagged along.

We were waiting at the ticket counter on platform no. 1. I introduced Amit and Neha to all the others. We had to get down at CST and from there we decided to go to Chowpatty by taxi.

'Amit, do you booze?' Swapnil asked. There was no need for him to ask this question now. I nudged Swapnil lightly and told him to shut up. But he did not listen. He asked Amit the same question again.

'No, I don't even smoke,' Amit said resting his hand on Neha's shoulder.

'Good man. You seem to be a real mamma's boy,' Anup added. I was now enjoying his leg pulling so I did not stop my friends.

Neha felt the need to defend her boyfriend in front of everyone and said, 'He is my Amit. He will never do things I don't approve of.'

Amit gave me a look of 'See, I'm ready to do anything for her'. The leg pulling continued till we reached CST. We came out of the station and started looking for taxis. Amit and Neha hired one taxi and the rest of us took another. We reached Chowpatty within a few minutes.

Everyone, including me, started shouting in joy, almost as if they were seeing the beach for the first time in life. However, with friends it is a different experience altogether. We sat on the beach. I was not interested in going into the water. Mumbai beaches are not as clean as they used to be earlier. I preferred eating chaat and my other favourite, paav bhaaji. Amit and Riya joined me. Neha and the others were near the water.

'Amit, what will you have?' Riya asked him.

'Nothing. I don't like junk food.'

I knew he would say something like this. I took out all my frustration on him.

'Abey behenchod , are you insane? Or are you crazy? Are you a Gladrags winner or are you Salman Khan? What's wrong with you? Why can't you eat paav bhaaji like the rest of us?'

Riya was shocked to see me shouting at Amit like this. We looked at each other and burst out laughing. We had paav bhaaji and pani puri. Riya to have ice cream . I wondered why all girls were so crazy about ice cream. Maybe they liked wasting their boyfriend's money.

'Hey Amit, come here. Let's go for a walk,' Neha shouted from afar.

'Thank God she knows I exist. I thought she was just going to enjoy by herself and then we would leave,' said Amit in anger. I could tell how low Amit must be feeling. Riya egged Amit to go. Once he left, both of us were on our own. Swapnil and Anup were nowhere to be seen. I thought they had gone for a smoke somewhere. Even I felt like taking a smoke break. However, since Riya was with me, I ignored the temptation.

Riya and I went for a long walk. Holding hands, looking at each other, leaving the world behind. I was walking so close to her that we hardly had any space in between us.

'Jaan, how much do you love me?' Riya asked me.

I went down on my knees and said, 'Last time, I had proposed to you in front of five other people. Today I will propose to you in front of a thousand people. I love you and this love is growing rapidly each day. Your touch still sends shivers down my body. Every kiss feels like our first kiss. I love you. I love your luscious lips. I love your caring nature.' We hugged each other.

We left after sometime. Neha and Riya wanted to go to Colaba for shopping. It was around 3 pm. We tried to convince them that Nariman Point was too far.

However, who could argue with girls. Finally, we decided to go by taxi. We reached the place after some time.

Colaba had many small shops where we could get anything—from shoes and sandals to clothes. Riya wanted to buy chappals while Neha wanted to buy shoes.

'Jaan, please make it fast. I hate walking for no reason,' I said to Riya.

Riya gave me an angry look and kept on walking. We went to a few shops but the girls did not like anything. We boys decided to go somewhere else. We told Neha and Riya that they could continue shopping, and we would join them in sometime. We stopped near a tapri.

'Amit, you really don't smoke or did you say it because Neha was there with you?' Anup asked him.

'I am serious. I have never tried it and do not want to try it ever in my life,' he replied.

'Superb yaar. Why do you require money then? No smoking. No boozing. No junk food. Neha has got the cheapest boyfriend in the city,' said Swapnil and we all laughed.

'Amit, what's your first semester result?' Swapnil asked him.

'Three KTs. BEE, Mechanics, and Maths 1.'

'How can you get a KT? I mean you must be attending college and classes regularly,' Anup said.

'Oh, stop it yaar. Stop talking about fucking engineering,' I said.

After some time, Riya called me and said that they were

done with shopping. I loved the chappals she had bought for herself. She had also bought a T-shirt for me.

'Thank you jaan. I love you a lot,' I said giving her a slight peck on the cheek.

We went to McDonald's and had a burger each. It was 6 pm by the time we decided to leave.

'How are we going?' Amit asked.

'Do one thing— you all can take the train while Riya and I will come by taxi.' I looked at Riya and she looked back at me in surprise. I just wanted to be alone with her. I wanted to end the day by spending some quality time with her.

Once all the others had left, Riya asked me, 'Any more surprise?' 'No jaan. I just wanted us to be together. Just us,' I said calling out for a taxi. A cab stopped in front of us. I took the bag from her hand and sat in the taxi. I kept the plastic bag behind.

'Hey, do you want this taxi driver to come to your house and tell your mom that you were roaming around with me?'Riya said.

'Don't worry. I won't forget it this time,' I said referring to the bag kept at the back. Riya started asking me about our future.

'Jaan, I want to marry you,' she said kissing me on my lips.

Marriage? This early in life? I had known from the first day itself that we were moving rather quickly. How could I marry so early?

'Jaan please,' she requested me.

'Have you lost it? What marriage are you talking about? Is this a joke? It's not funny.'

'Do you mean you will not marry me? Is that so?' she said shouting at me. How could I make her understand this was not funny.

I decided that I did not want to end the day with a fight. I told the driver to take us to Dadar.

'Why Dadar? It's so late Aadi…'

'Shut up and don't argue,' I said kissing her on the lips. That was the best way to shut her up.

We reached Dadar. I gave the driver the fare and asked Riya to walk along with me. We were near the plaza bus stop. I told her we were going to Siddhivinayak temple.

"Now? We could have come some days later. What is the urge to go now? What is going on in your mind?'

'We are going to get married,' I said. She went blank. 'Jaan…I did not really mean what I had said earlier. How can we marry?'

'Why, don't you want to marry me now? If you do, then come along with me. This won't be a legal marriage. However, we will take seven promises in front of the God as is done in any marriage. Saat phere. I have decided what will be the seven promises. Are you ready?'

She kept on looking at me for sometime and then broke into a huge smile. In a matter of a few minutes, we had both matured into young adults. We reached Siddhivinayak temple. Once inside, we took God's blessings. The temple's pandits do not allow anyone to stand near the idol for more than ten seconds. Once our time was up, they just pushed us away. We went to one secluded corner of the temple. I asked for her permission to start and told her to remove her gold necklace.

I said, 'We will make 7 promises in front of God. Then we will unofficially be husband and wife. Is that fine?'

She agreed. I took her hand in mine.

Continuing with our vows, I said, 'Promise 1. We will always be together. Let's promise we will never leave each other. Promise me we will always be together. Whatever be the situation, we will never leave each other alone.'

'I promise you Aadi, I won't leave you. I will always be with you like your shadow. A shadow which will be with you after sunset too. I will never disappear,' she replied.

'Promise 2. We will never fight. We promise that if we go wrong in some decision or have minor disagreements in the future, we won't fight. We will always love each other and make each other smile.'

'I promise Aadi… I will never fight. Even if I think of fighting, I will stop talking to you but won't fight. I can't handle fights between us. We will always love each other.'

'Promise 3. We will not let our love fade. Promise me that even after spending years together we won't take each other for granted. We will still have warmth in our relationship. We will never let our love fade. Whenever we feel our love is fading, promise me you will close your eyes and think of all the good times we spent in past.'

'I promise Aadi… I won't let our love fade. This will never happen. Going away from you is not in my destiny. I do not want to change my destiny.'

'Promise 4. We will always trust each other. Promise me whenever you feel I am hanging out with someone else or lying to you, you will put that thought out of your mind. You will always trust me. I promise it.'

'I promise Aadi… I will never spy on you. I will never point a finger towards you. I will always trust you.'

'Promise 5. We will always respect each other. Promise me we will always respect each other in public or private. Promise me you will never shout at me. Promise me that you will always respect me. I promise to do the same.'

'I promise Aadi… I will always respect you. I promise to listen to whatever you say. I will never hurt you in public or private.'

'Promise no. 6. We will never bring our past between us. I promise I will never bring our past in our relationship. I do not mind whatever your past was. I don't care about it. However, I won't let it affect our relationship. I will never ask you about your past.'

'I promise Aadi… I too will never ask you about your past. I will forget everything about your past. Your previous relationships. I just want you in my present and future.'

'Promise no. 7: We will not neglect our studies. I promise I will never neglect my studies. I promise I will concentrate on studies and clear engineering. I promise I will never sidetrack from studies.'

'This is not fair. Still, I promise I will complete my engineering and get placed in some good company.'

I put the gold necklace round her neck. She cried in joy. This is the moment a girl waits for all her life. This is the moment which comes once in a lifetime. But we would be lucky to do it twice. We were standing together in front of God, happy after making so many promises. Even God would have had no choice but to accept us. We had taken one more step ahead in our relationship.

Aditya and Riya were married—unofficially.

The Beginning of the End

It was exam time again. This time I wanted to study well and secure good marks. The second half of the year is always more dangerous than the first. I had heard of numerous cases of students dropping out in the second half after being unable to cope up with the demands of the subject. I was almost done with my preparations in every subject including solving the first semester papers. Even Riya had studied hard this time. We wanted to show our folks at home that we were not going to let our relationship affect our studies. And Riya had promised my mom that she would make sure I studied hard. This time even the submission went off smoothly. This further boosted my confidence. I wanted to show mom how special Riya was for me and what a difference she made in my life. Soon it was time to write our last paper—Maths 2. it was the toughest paper in the second semester. But I wasn't worried since I was going in fully prepared. I knew differential equation and rectifications by heart now and was confident of passing the exam. We had decided to drink the whole night after the paper to celebrate.

The paper was extremely tough. Still I tried to answer as many questions as I could. One by one, all of us trickled out of the classroom.

'I can't believe it's the end of one year in engineering. We will be promoted to the second year,' said Anup.

'Seriously yaar, even I can't believe it's the end of our first year here. Let's get naughty tonight and drink and party.' This was the first time I was going to drink. I had never touched beer before. I was nervous and excited. I had no guilty feelings this time. I was in a mood to party after having made it through a difficult first year.

I did not allow Riya and the other girls to join us in the festivities. If we had taken girls along, Pop Tate's Restro Bar would have been the only option nearby and we boys wanted strong beer and not mocktails. After all, we had successfully made through one year of engineering.

'Bachcha, drink within limits. I don't want it to become a habit. Please promise me you won't drink too much,' said Riya.

'Okay sweetheart, I won't. Promise.'

I promised Riya that I would meet her a day later. She didn't seem to mind and gave me permission to carry on. I told everyone at home that I was going to spend the night at Sameer's place. Our plan was to drink until 1 am and then spend the night at Sameer's house since his parents were going to be away for two days. It was going to be a night of fun, a night when I would have my first drink.

We left from our respective houses at around 7 pm. We all decided to meet outside Mamta bar. Sameer, Anup, and Swapnil were already there by the time I reached. Once in, we ordered two beers and a few snacks. The waiter poured beer into my glass. It was going to be my life's first glass of beer. I was afraid of facing the consequences. I kept asking myself, Should I or shouldn't I? I was confused. But I had worked hard all year and wanted to enjoy myself.

'Cheers,' everyone said loudly.

'Cheers to the end of one year,' Anup said raising his glass.

I took my first sip of beer. It tasted awful. I quickly chewed a few cashew nuts. Everyone was staring at me, probably thinking what a wuss I was.

'Relax guys. I'll finish it. Don't worry,' I assured them.

One glass down, my eyes started becoming heavy and I was beginning to lose control over my body. We ordered two more beers. I was partially stable and enjoying myself with a beer in one hand and a cigarette in the other.

'Waiter, two more beers and a full chicken tandoori,' Swapnil screamed since the music was playing at full blast on his mobile.

'Hey, enough now,' I said to everyone trying to keep my eyes open.

'Oh come on, Aadi...have just one more glass.'

After much coaxing, I gave in to their demands and called for another glass of beer with tandoori chicken. And another one. And so it continued till I was almost ten glasses down. By the end of it, I was totally out of my mind.

'Aadi...Riya had told you not to drink so much. You had promised her you will drink within limits,' said Sameer shaking me up.

'Please, get away from me. Let me relax,' I said almost about to puke. Sameer was holding on to me or I would have fallen flat on the table.

'Aadi, shall I call Riya and tell her what you are upto?' Sameer said angrily.

'Mind your own business, Sameer. You can't blackmail me by taking Riya's name. I don't care. Do whatever you want to.'

Sameer called Riya up and told her everything. Five minutes later, I got a call from her.

'Hi jaan...what do you want? Why are you calling me at this hour? So you trust Sameer so much that you are willing to believe whatever he tells you? Well, he's lying. I am not all that drunk. So don't worry, I'll be fine. I know how to take care of myself,' I said groggily.

I was so heavily intoxicated that I couldn't even catch what she was saying. The phone slipped from my hand

and I fell on the table into a deep slumber. Sameer tried to wake me up. Anup splashed water on my face. Both of them hauled me up and took me out of the bar.

After making me sit on the footpath, Swapnil shouted, 'Are you an idiot? How were you talking to Riya?'

'Excuse me? She is my girlfriend. Or have you started loving her too? Tell me, do you also want her?' I did not know what I was saying. The words were just coming out of my mouth.

Sameer slapped me hard on my face. I fell down on the footpath. I do not remember anything after that.

Second Year

It was not a happy start to the second year. The next day when I went to see the notice board in college to check which division and roll number I had been allotted, I found that Riya was no longer in my class. That meant we could only meet in between breaks. I had come late to college. Riya was already attending her lecture. She had messaged me a few minutes ago asking me when I was coming. When I peeped into my new classroom, to my horror I saw that there were all new faces. My eyes were searching for Riya. I took my seat in the last row and stared continuously at the third row where Riya used to sit.

But Riya was missing this time. The entire first year was spent in watching her during lectures. I took my mobile and gave her a missed call. Again my eyes went to the third row. Riya used to look back whenever I would give a missed call. I was missing everything. I was missing all the moments that we shared in the first year. This was really painful. I messaged her but she did not reply. Maybe she is sitting on the first bench, I thought. This upset me even more. I wanted to see her so badly. I hadn't talked to her once all morning and was longing to hear her voice. This was not the morning I had wished for. It was not what I wanted. I wanted her. I enjoyed going to college only because she was with me. But now what?

As I was about to call her again, I got a message from her.

```
Where are you bachcha? Have you reached
college.? I am in the middle of a lecture. Will
meet you during break time.
```

I replied immediately.

```
Miss you jaan. I'm in the lecture hall. My eyes
are fixed on the third row where you used to
sit. You're not there anymore. :(
```

I was waiting for her to reply but she did not. How was I going to sit alone in this classroom? How could I attend lectures without her? How could I concentrate? How could I laugh during lectures? We had been separated for no reason. We did not like it but we had to put up with it. I was not comfortable with all the new faces around me. There was no Swapnil nor Anup. They were both in the IT section with Riya. Even Sameer was not here with me. This made lectures even tougher for me to bear.

I looked at my watch. There were still twenty minutes left for the lecture to end. It was like time had come to a standstill. Each minute seemed like months to me. When I was with Riya, time would just fly. Now I was all alone.

I called Riya up as soon as the professor left the class. It was 1.30 pm. Time for a much-needed break. Riya didn't pick up the call. I went and stood outside her class which was on the third floor. The lecture was still in progress. I waited impatiently outside and as soon as the professor came out, I ran into the classroom. Swapnil and Riya were sitting together. I could not spot Anup anywhere. I did not care. I wanted my sweetheart beside me. I called out to her. She was so happy to see me! Both of us had tears in our eyes. It was afternoon and we had not even seen each once since morning.

'I missed you jaan. Not seeing you in class brought back all the memories of the first year. I miss how you would turn from the third row when I would call out your name. I miss seeing your smile. I miss your messages. Your missed calls. Being without you is tough, jaan. How can I survive in that class? It kills me not seeing you there.' I was holding her hands tight.

'Even I miss you. I miss your naughty smiles and the little things that you used to do for me. And even I looked back a few times during the lecture but found you nowhere. Love you. Should we go and grab a bite to eat? I have brought along your favourite—rajma chawal.'

She opened her tiffin box and put a spoonful of rice in my mouth.

'Hey Swapnil, where is Anup? I miss you people. The first year with all of you was superb. It's going to be difficult for me now,' I said to Swapnil.

'He has gone out with a friend. Had some work, I think. We will miss you too, Aadi. Especially Riya. She has been upset since morning. Why don't you take her out somewhere,' Swapnil said patting my back.

Sameer came shouting into the room, 'Hey guys, the result is displayed. Let's go and check.'

Every semester result brings with it a sense of apprehension. We were not confident about our results. We left the class immediately and reached the library outside which the results had been displayed. Sameer somehow managed to go near the board. We asked him to look for our names too. He came out of the rush and was looking upset.

'What happened? Did you check the results?' I asked him. We all were looking at him.

'Yes, I have got 4 KTs in the second semester and 1 KT in the first semester. I have been dropped for a year,' he said almost on the verge of tears.

This made our hearts pump abruptly. I could not believe Sameer had been dropped. I searched for my name in the result sheet. I had managed to pass in all subjects in the first semester! Even Riya had passed all of hers. So had Swapnil. Anup had got 1 KT. I still could not look for my name on the second semester result. I was really tensed because of Sameer's result. Finally, I saw my name. One KT in Maths 2. I could not believe it. Maths was one subject I was good in. I had scored 95 marks in HSC and 68 in Maths 1. Mumbai Univerrsity—totally unpredictable.

I saw Riya's result. She had got 1 KT in BEE. Swapnil and Anup had passed.

'Hey Sameer, don't worry. we will do something. Just chill,' I consoled him.

'I cannot believe I have failed. My papers were not so bad. So how have I scored in 30s? Mumbai University sucks yaar! They don't show any kindness towards students. This is the most fucked up university ever,' Sameer cried out in frustration.

'Don't worry. Give your papers for rechecking. Maybe it was a mistake on their part,' Riya said to Sameer.

We bunked the next few classes and left home early that day. My parents were happy with my result. I was officially in the second year now. But I still could not believe how I could have got 1 KT in Maths 2. Maybe Sameer was right after all. College sucks.

Dad gave me permission to take my Honda Activa to college from thereon. It was getting boring going by train everyday. Having one's own vehicle is always better for it is time saving and hassle free. Even Riya's parents were ready to purchase a new two-wheeler for her. She wanted to buy a Scooty Pep. She asked me which colour would look nice. I told her to buy one in red, my favourite. A red hot and spicy girl on a red Scooty Pep. The only thing that was killing me was that I could not be with Riya during the lectures.

The seniors had warned us that the second year Electronics branch was the worst branch in college. They had also warned us about a particular professor who was very strict. Shinde sir. He taught Electronics Design. ECAD 1. The subject was very complicated. Our seniors had told us to attend as many of Shinde sir's lectures as we could.

We were sitting in class for Shinde sir's first lecture when he entered the classroom. He was on the shorter side. Formally dressed, a folder in his hand, he entered the class as if he was the king of the college. Plus, he had a big belly that was portruding from his shirt. Everybody stood up to greet him in unison. He placed the folder on the table and started taking our attendance.

'Listen up everybody. I won't manipulate the attendance at the end of semester. So try and attend the maximum number of lectures you can. Those who have less than 75 percent attendance won't be allowed to make their final submissions. The rest is up to you. So let's start with the subject,' he said.

His warning made me think twice. His voice had such an impact that there was pin drop silence in the classroom. No one uttered a single word throughout the lecture. For the next one hour that he taught us, he did not smile even once. But he taught us well. The best I had seen so far since last year. Nevertheless, I knew he would kick our asses if we were not regular. I met Riya after the class and told her about Shinde sir.

We decided to go for a walk in the campus lawns. 'Riya, I have been thinking about something since the last few days and wanted to share it with you now,' I said.

'What is it? Is there any problem?' Riya was staring at me.

'There's no problem as such. I was thinking we should concentrate on our studies now. It's the second year. And now that we have enrolled ourselves into this fucking engineering course, let's do it seriously. We can't look back now; let us study hard before it gets too late. I am not saying we will stop meeting or anything, but just that we should devote more time to our studies.'

'I think you are right. Even I was thinking about this. But the truth is that I cannot live without meeting you or spending some time with you.'

We decided to start studying regularly from that day onwards. I was more regular than Riya. We used to meet before and after college, as well as in between breaks. But gradually things changed. Earlier I used to bunk my last lecture and meet her. But with the pressure of studies looming large over our heads, our meetings turned into a rarity.

Our Head of Department changed the timetable and shifted Shinde sir's lecture from 5 pm to 6 pm. This made my life worse. I used to come to college in the morning for practicals that went on till 6 in the evening. Riya was initially upset when she found out about my revised timings, but she did not say anything. I convinced her by saying that I would meet her after college until 7 pm and then go home. That calmed her down a bit.

It was tough for me too. Last year, Riya and I were together all day long. From morning till evening. Even after college we used to be together for an hour. But this was getting impossible now. We could hardly manage a few minutes together.

I used to reach home around 7.30 pm. For two days a week I had classes at 7 pm. On those days we could not meet at all. The schedule became too hectic for me to handle. I used to be extremely stressed out by the end of the day. Riya and I tried to steal a few minutes with each other by talking on the phone at night. She used to call me around 11 pm after our parents had retired to bed. But sometimes I would be so tired by the end of the day that I would forget to take her call.

'Aadi…this is too much. I can't handle this,' Riya complained one day. You have to talk to me today. I do not want to listen to a single excuse. I don't care if you are tired. Please Aadi…I love you. This is really difficult. I am so used to listening to your voice and having you around. I am used to your touches, your sweet talk. Please.'

'I know jaan. Even I can't do without talking to you. But I get so tired by the time I return home that I fall asleep as soon as I put my head on the pillow. But I promise not to do that today.'

After about 30 minutes, I told her that I was feeling sleepy.

'Fine. You don't want to talk to me. Go to hell! I am mad to love you so much. Even I am tired Aadi… You think as if you are the only one attending lectures. It's not like I'm sitting at home and doing nothing. Why do you create so much hype out of small things? I don't get to see you or talk to you in the mornings, but now you don't want to talk during the night as well. Fine then. Get lost. Bye. I hate you!' It was the first time I had seen her so angry.

She was not wrong on her part, but I couldn't do anything about it. I was not used to this schedule. Attending lectures without Riya was boring. Even Sameer and the rest of the gang was missing.

I fell asleep as soon as she put the phone down. I could not keep my eyes open. Everything was getting worse. Everything seemed to be different. I got up in the morning and checked my cellphone. The screen flashed 26 missed calls and 8 new messages.

Oh, shit! I thought Riya had gone to sleep last night. I should have waited for her call. But I didn't. Now it would culminate in a big fight. I checked that her last call had come at 4.30 am and her last message was sent at 4.40 am. I checked the time on the wall clock. It was 9 am. I immediately called her up and heard an automated voice say, 'The mobile you are trying to reach is currently switched off.'

I knew she was angry. I became tensed and prayed for everything to be okay. I kept on calling her but there was no response. Dejected, I left home for college. I tried my luck again after reaching college and called her one more time before my first class. This time she picked up the phone.

'Hey jaan…my wife…I am so, so sorry. I thought you had slept yesterday. Forgive me. This will never happen again,' I pleaded with her admitting my mistake.

'Let it be, Aadi. Keep the phone down. I don't want to talk to you,' she said in anger.

'Please jaan. I…' Before I could finish the sentence, she disconnected the call.

I called her again but she did not pick up the call. I went to her classroom and saw her sitting in a corner with a sad face. The lecture had not started yet. I somehow convinced her to come out of the classroom and talk to me. But she started looking in some other direction. I was continuously apologizing to her. But she was so angry, she didn't pay any heed to my apologies. Finally, I took her bag from the classroom and started walking away.

'Aadi… what are you doing? I do not want to go anywhere. Please,' she said running after me.

I stopped and smiled at her. But she was in no mood to smile and bit her lower lip in anger. I loved her in that mood too.

'This angry look of yours suits you,' I said pinching her cheeks. She reluctantly started walking beside me but didn't talk. We were walking towards the bus stop. I thought of calling Amit and Neha to come along with us. I knew Riya would not talk to me if it was just the two of us. I called up Amit and asked him, 'Are you free?'

'I am with Neha in Aerol. What happened? Any work?' he replied.

'I am going to Grant Lane with Riya. Do you want to join us?' I looked at Riya. She gave me a what-do-you-think-you-are-doing look. I kissed her cheeks. She still looked as angry as before.

Amit agreed to come along with Neha. By the time they came, I was still trying my best to convince Riya to let go and not be a spoilsport. But it was of no use. I told Neha to have a word with Riya. I had messaged Amit about our fight and he knew everything that was happening. Amit and I went to get water, giving Neha time to talk to Riya while we were gone. By the time we came back, I was really happy to see a smile on Riya's face. Neha had succeeded in convincing her. I hugged her tightly in front of them. I was in seventh heaven when I saw her smile. I could have died a thousand deaths for that smile. It felt extremely good to patch up after so long. She kissed me on my cheek and said sorry. I was in tears.

'Please jaan… Never do something like this again. I can't live without you. Please. You don't know what was going through in my heart all this while. I really love you a lot. I am sorry, I won't ever do something like this again. Love you.'

'Will I hurt you? Nah, never. Love you? Forever. Defend you? In every heartbeat. Hate you? Impossible.'

We went and sat in the garden. A passsionate kiss after a big fight felt really good. Fondling each other after a fight was better. Feeling each other up after a fight was the best. Romance was in the air.

'Jaan…I thought I had lost you. I was really tensed. Please let's not get angry with each other ever again,' I said and put my head on her lap.

'Bachcha, what are you so afraid of? Don't forget that we are married now. I can't leave you. We had taken a vow of never fighting with each other and I broke the second promise today. I am really sorry. But I did not have any other method of getting your attention. You never listen to anyone unless a proof is provided to you. I am sorry. You think you're the only one who cried? I was crying all of last night. I love you more than you love me.'

She is an angel, I thought. She had made my day by saying this. Love you my sweetheart.

Neha and Amit, who had gone off to grab a bite at the nearest dhaba, came and joined us.

'Done with your fights?' Amit asked looking at Riya.

'Yes it's over. We've realized we can't live without each other,' Riya replied.

'Aadi...you have changed Riya. She was not like this in school. You have seriously changed her a lot,' Amit said looking at Neha and laughed.

'What do you mean I have changed her? She has changed me. Had she not been there, I would have left engineering for sure,' I said.

'She was very mischievous in school. I remember many of my friends used to like her. However, she never cared for anyone except that guy...what was his name Riya?' Amit asked.

'I don't remember. What are you talking about? I never 'cared for' anyone. You must have been mistaken,' Riya replied almost apologetically, like she had done something wrong and had been caught red handed.

'Remember our class picnic to Alibagh? The time when you went out for a walk on the beach with that guy. You had slept on his lap all through the night. Remember?' Amit asked.

Riya and I were staring at each other. What was Amit talking about? Riya had never mentioned anything like this before. She had slept on someone's lap for the whole night at Alibagh beach! What was I hearing?

'What are you saying, Amit. You're joking, right?' I wanted him to say he was joking.

'I am dead serious man. I thought Riya had told you about this. Anyway forget it. Let's leave. It's getting late,' said Amit giving me an apologetic look, that told me he was sorry for what he had blurted out by mistake. He told me not to make this an issue to fight on. However, I couldn't stop myself. Amit and Neha were walking ahead of us.

'What is this Riya? You slept with someone? For the whole night? Did you think I will never get to know about this and it will be forgotten? ' I was losing my mind over this.

'Bachcha...I never slept with anyone. Are you mad? I am only yours. How can I do such a thing? I had rested my head on his lap for merely five minutes. He is like a brother to me.'

'I don't care about that. Who is he? Why did you hide this from me? You should have told me that you slept with him.'

'Are you mad? I am telling you I did not sleep with anyone and you're saying I should have told you. He is like my cousin. I didn't have any feelings for him.'

I did not want to fight with her at that moment. She was almost on the verge of tears. I could not see her crying, so I changed the topic and pulled her closer to me. She rested her head on my shoulders in the bus and dozed off. I kept running my fingers through her hair. A million thoughts were running in my mind. Things were getting worse. Lectures, classes, no time to meet, no time to call each other and talk for hours, frequent fights, and now this talk of her having slept with someone else. I decided to break all the promises I had taken with her in Siddhivinayak temple. I wanted to see if I could live without Riya. I loved her. However, I wanted to test myself. I wanted to test my fate. It was decided then—I was going to break up with Riya. Maybe it was the worst decision I could take but I did take it.

Can't Be Separated

There is nothing more difficult than breaking up a relationship. What had begun with mutual attraction, followed by excitement and joy, had somewhere along the way turned out to be the reason for my discomfort. Whatever the reasons, it was enough for me to conclude that breaking up was the only thing left to do. To be the one whose decision it was to break up in the first place is a very difficult position to be in. It made me feel guilty, like I was going to do something very wrong. But every good thing must come to an end. Maybe ours was a hot, torrid, quick love that could only last till here and no more.

I messaged her.

Jaan, I love you. You can't imagine how much I care for you; you provided direction to my life. However, a few disputes in the recent past have hurt me a lot. I tried to move on but can't. I feel that the charm we had before is missing now. I have made a decision. I think we both should give ourselves some time to be

```
alone. I am not saying I won't talk to you or
message you. But we should take a break. It's
time to think over it and see can if we can
really clive without each other or not. I am
sorry. Please take care of yourself.
```

She immediately called me. I avoided her call. My heart was crying but I had to do this. I was trying hard to go away from her. I wanted to see whether I could live without her or not. I was thinking of the night in Alibagh and what might have happened.

She was continuously calling and messaging. One of her messages brought tears in my eyes:

```
You used to say that your heart skips a beat
when you see me, feel my touch, when I speak,
when I smile. So what has happened to you now?
Even my heart used to skip a beat when I used
to see you. However, that one beat will give
me a lifetime of tears now. I will never love
again. I will never trust anyone again. I will
always love you and wait for you. Miss you.
Your so called bachcha. Your unofficial wife.
Saying you final goodbye by kissing your ring.
```

I replied to her again.

```
Please do not cry jaan. For me at least. I have
not gone too far. I am still with you. Just
give me some time. Love you. Miss you.
```

When she came into my classroom the next morning, I could see her eyes were swollen. She must have cried the whole night. She still had tears in her eyes. I was feeling more guilty now. I told her not to cry. I wiped her tears. That made her cry even more. I played with her cheeks. And I saw a weak smile on her face. I again told her to give me few days to think over it.

I wanted to tell everybody what had happened. I messaged Swapnil and the others to bunk the lecture and come to Aerol station. Once all of them came, I told them everything that had happened in last few days—our fights, the night out at Alibagh, and every other small detail. Finally, I told them that I had broken up.

Swapnil came to me and slapped me as hard as he could. I was shocked for a few minutes. Nobody spoke a word.

'I had warned you in the beginning itself. She is a nice girl. She is like my sister. How dare you take this decision? She loves you so much and you are acting like a fool. You must have slept with her. Now you need someone else, right?' Swapnil shouted.

'It's not that, yaar. You have misunderstood me. I still love her but I need more time to think it over. But you will never understand all this. I am leaving,' I said and started walking back home. I was more upset now. I thought at least my friends would support me. But it didn't seem like they would. I thought I had taken the wrong decision. But I couldn't handle it now. She was calling me continuously on my way back home. I did not pick up a single call. I was more hurt than anyone else. However, no one understood why I was asking for time to think. My love for her was increasing day by day. I just wanted a few more days' time to find out if it was really love or not.

I reached home. My phone was continuously vibrating. I lied down on my bed and checked my missed calls. I saw there were two missed calls from Neha and one from Amit. Riya must have told them about our breakup. I called Amit.

'Hey Aadi… have you lost your mind? Why are you hurting Riya? She loves you so much. And as far as I know, so do you. Then why are you both hurting each other? You will leave her just because you think she slept with someone else in Alibagh?' screamed Amit over the phone.

He continued, 'She didn't sleep with anyone. She just rested her head on his lap. She did not sleep with anyone. Do you get me? And who are you to say she slept with someone?' I kept the phone down and called Neha. She sounded tense. I asked her what was wrong.

'Aadi, Riya had called up Amit when we were in Grant Lane. She was crying a lot. She told him everything that had happened between you guys. Amit was quite disturbed. He went away and spoke to her for almost 15 minutes. Then he came back with a smile on his face. I wonder what he told her,' said Neha crying.

How foolish is this girl, I thought to myself. I am going through such a bad phase and she has to bring her own personal issues to the fore. Amit and I were good friends so he must have told Riya how much I loved her, nothing else. I did not know what to tell Neha. So I kept the phone down. It did not seem important to me. It was anyways not a big issue for me. Amit went away and had a word with Riya. What's wrong in that? I wished Neha was in front of me. I would have killed her. Idiot!

I received a call from Riya. I picked the call. She did not say a single word. She was crying continuously. I did not keep the phone down. It would have been an insult to her. She was disappointed and did not know what to say. She played our favourite song in the background. It brought tears in my eyes. It was the same song we used to sing for each other. The same song on which we used to kiss each other, smile at each other. But today with the same song playing, we were crying. I wanted to kill myself. I could not bear any of this. I pleaded with Riya to stop crying. But she didn't. I had to keep the phone down. She called back again. I did not pick up. I received one message from her saying goodbye. Tears rolled down my face. Just when I thought that the dam I had built around my heart to keep the pain at bay would hold strong, it sprang a leak. Eating away at the aching pieces until it was torn down...and your eyes were nothing more than fountains of bitter tears that drained you of all emotion leaving you hollow and desolate inside.

And strangely enough, I knew all this was going to happen. But no one told me it could hurt so much. My heart ached. I could not bear this anymore. I picked up the phone and called her.

'*Tujhe dekh dekh sona…tujhe dekh kar hai jagna…*' I cried and cried. I couldn't sing any more. She continued with the song. We cried the whole night on phone. By morning we had decided to give our relationship one more chance.

A Bitter Ending

We were enjoying a new phase of our relationship, the thrill of being together again after so long. Amit and Neha had also become good friends with us and we would hang out together quite often. Amit in particularly had become really good friends with me. We used to call each other up frequently. I started liking him as a friend. He used to ask me about my relationship and whatever was happening in my life. He helped me –in work and in love.

Mom came up to me one Saturday and said, 'Aadi, tomorrow we have to go to Ratnagiri for a few days. Some important work has to come up and you need to come along with me. So inform your class professor and take a few days off.'

I had a Maths class in Aerol that day. After classes the four of us used to hang out together along with Swapnil. Swapnil was happy seeing Riya and me together again. He used to care a lot for her. He apologized to me for the slap. I was sitting besides Riya in the class writing love messages on her notebook. It felt nice being back with her again. I also wanted to take studies seriously and attend lectures regularly. But I knew I could not do all this without Riya by my side. I studied for her. I attended lectures for her. I loved her like crazy.

After the class got over, I told Riya that I was leaving for Ratnagiri and would be back in a few days. She seemed sad that I would be gone for some days and she would have to stay without me. I kissed her on her cheeks and told her how much I loved her.

'I will miss you a lot, jaan. If Dad had not been there I would have told you to come along with us as well. Love you. Miss you,' I said holding her hands tightly.

We spent some time together after which I left for home. Early next morning we left for Ratnagiri. I messaged Riya before leaving:

Jaan, it will take me four days to return. Love you. Will miss you.

After some time I got a reply from her: Miss you too.

Four days seemed like a lot without her. I was not able to concentrate on anything. I wanted to get back home as quickly as possible. I wanted to look into Riya's eyes. I wanted to feel her touch. I wanted to make her smile. I wanted to hear her voice. I called her once or twice but she didn't pick up the call. The place where I was staying did not have good network coverage.

Maybe she did try calling me but the call did not get through because of bad network. By the end of the trip, I was missing her a lot.

The work that we had come for was almost done. It was our last day in Ratnagiri.

I messaged her saying:

```
When our song comes on the radio, I can't help
thinking of you and I start crying. When I go
to bed at night, I cry because I miss you so
much. Jaan I need you.

  I want to see you. It's been four days and
it feels like four weeks. I love you so much.
I am leaving now. I will be back tomorrow
morning. I hope you are as excited to see me
as I am.
```

I wanted to be with her that very moment. But she was miles away. I wished she could call me and make my day better.

Nothing would be more beautiful than hearing her voice. But I could not complain as the mobile network was weak.

My folks and I reached home early next morning. I had slept for only three hours and retired to bed to catch a quick nap. I called Riya the minute I got up. But she did not pick up my call. I tried calling her again. No reply. I messaged her saying I was back and wanted to meet, but did not get a reply for my message. I was afraid. What had happened while I was gone? I decided to check up on her without informing her in advance. I could not wait to see her face. I wanted to see her smile. I drove my Activa almost at full speed and reached Aerol. I called her again, but she did not pick up my phone. Maybe she's in college, I thought. I went straight to college. I looked for her everywhere in the campus but could not find her. I called up Swapnil.

'Have you seen Riya? Did she came to college?'

'No. She hasn't been coming to college—neither today nor yesterday. She came only on Monday and Tuesday. Is there a problem?' Swapnil asked me.

'Nothing serious. I am back after my trip and have been trying to contact her. But she is not picking up my call. She hasn't even been replying to my messages. That's why I thought she must be in college.'

I disconnected the call and came outside the college. Once outside, I called her up again. She finally picked up my call.

'Where are you?' she asked me in very low voice.

'I have just reached Mumbai. I have been trying to call you since a long time. Where are you?' I asked her in a tense voice.

'I am in the middle of a lecture. Why don't you come to college directly? When are you coming? I will meet you after college. I have practicals now. Sorry. Bye,' she said and kept the phone down.

I had been in college a few minutes back. I had looked for her everywhere. I had checked her classroom and confirmed with Swapnil. Why was she lying to me? I was confused. I called up Swapnil again.

'Swapnil, are you sure Riya is not in college? Did you check in the lecture hall? She must be in class,' I asked him.

'No, she is not in college. I was present for the last lecture. She was not there. I thought you had found her and she was with you,' Swapnil said.

'She told me she was in a lecture and practicals and that she will meet me in the evening,' I said.

'She must be joking for sure. Maybe she wants to give you some sort of a surprise. Good luck buddy,' he said and kept the phone down.

This could be a possibility. She must be planning a surprise for me since I had not been with her for so many days. The thought of a surprise excited me.

I called up Neha thinking that she might know about what was going on.

'Hey Neha, how are you? Where is my jaan? What planning is going on behind my back? A big surprise, huh?' I asked her.

'Aadi, I want to meet you now. Where are you? Come near sector 19. It's urgent,' Neha replied.

'Okay fine. Surprise in sector 19, is it? Superb. I am coming right now. I will reach in 5 minutes. Come soon. Bring my jaan also,' I kept the phone down and started for sector 19. When I reached there, I saw Neha standing alone. My eyes searched for Riya. When I asked Neha about Riya, she started crying. I asked her what the matter was.

'Aadi, Amit has been avoiding me since the past few days. From the day I shouted at him in Grant Lane when Riya called him, he has been treating me very badly. I am afraid I might lose him. Please do something Aadi. He will listen to you. Please.'

I wanted to meet Riya desperately and Neha was asking me to talk to Amit. This meant Neha did not know anything about the surprise. She was crying a lot. I could not see her crying like that. I called Amit. He did not take my call. I messaged him to call me back as soon as he got free. I asked Neha about Riya.

'I don't know where she is. I did not meet her after you went to Ratnagiri. I did not call her. I was not in the mood to talk to her. I was at home all through. But please talk to Amit. Please,' she cried again.

I calmed her down and left. I promised her I would talk to Amit, but even he was not taking my call. Nobody knew where Riya was. I called her again. Her cell was switched off. I was getting increasingly worried. I could not think of anything and told Neha to call at her home. Neha told me that her mom picked up the call and said Riya was in college. Now this was something unusual. Riya was not in college. Where could she be?

I went home. I was very upset with whatever had happened. I messaged her again.

Jaan where are you? I am tensed. Please reply. What has happened to you? I am sorry if I did something wrong. Please reply.

She sent me a reply saying: I am with my boyfriend. Ha ha…

I knew this was a joke and said: So how is your new boyfriend? Is he as hot as me?

Riya said: Yes. Not only is he hot, he is also an expert kisser.

I replied: Oh seriously? So you must be happy now. You got someone better than me. Congrats. Where are you now?

She said: I am in Grant Lane with him. Yes, he is better than you. He is sweet and does not make up excuses like you.

I replied: Stop joking jaan. I want to meet you. Where are you? I am in Aerol.

Riya said: I told you I am in Grant Lane with him. Meet you tomorrow morning. I will give you a big surprise.

I replied: Wow, I knew this. Thanks a lot. Even I have a small surprise for you. Miss you. I will come to Aerol tomorrow morning at 10 am. Then we will decide whether to attend college or not. Good night. Miss you. Love you. Muaah.

I couldn't sleep all night. I was eager to meet my sweetheart after so many days I decided to take chocolates for her and a greeting card that said 'Miss You'. I bought the best card available at the nearby gift shop. It said:

*I want to be in your arms where you hold me tight and
never let you go...*
I may be away but...
Even when we are far apart...
Distance can never change,
The love between us...
The love I have for you in my heart...
Love you always...

I reached Aerol and ran up to her and gave her a tight
hug. I was about to kiss her when she stopped me and
pushed me away. Her behaviour seemed a little odd.
She had never pushed me away before. I asked her what
had happened.

'I have a boyfriend now. Please don't do these things
in public,' she chided me.

I was shocked. What was she saying? Was she still
joking?

I asked her, 'Are you serious? Who is he?'

'Yes I am serious. I called you here for to tell you
precisely this.'

I could not handle it and started crying. I took out
my cell phone and called Swapnil. He did not pick up
the call. I called Sameer next. Thankfully he picked up.
I told him what Riya had said.

'Aadi, don't cry. Please, I request you. Please stop
crying. First listen to her and then call me back. Just
hear her out,' Sameer said and kept the phone down.

I could not stop crying. I thought she had done it on purpose.

'So what's his name?' I asked her.

'You want to know the name of my new boyfriend? He is better than you. He cares for me more than you ever could. Moreover, the most important thing is he loves me more than you. And I love him too.'

'Was he the reason you were not picking my call while I was away? And there I was thinking you were missing me,' I said.

'I did not miss you at all. He was with me all through. I tried calling you so many times. You want to know his name?' Riya said with a wicked smile on her face. 'His name is Amit. I like him. Maybe I love him...I don't know yet. He proposed to me a few days back and I accepted. We both like each other. Sorry Aadi... you hurt me a lot. And yes, we are in a relationship.'

'You are what?' I couldn't believe what I was hearing. 'I demand to know everything.'

'I'll tell you everything, provided you don't say a word in between.' And then she recounted her side of the story.

Riya's Confession

'Aditya—the man who came into my life and changed everything. Before I met you, I never knew what true love was. Though I admit I had liked a few people before, I had never 'loved' anyone. You were my first love. I realized why people go mad in love only after I met you. I still remember all our dates well—November 14, when you proposed to me; November 16, when we went out together for the first time; our first kiss, your first touch, all the sweet moments in central garden, each moment which we spent in Grant Lane, our engagement, our marriage, everything , everyday, every minute, every second—it was you in my mind and my heart. It was a dream come true for me.'

'However, as the days passed, I started noticing some sudden changes in you. I tried to ignore them at first, but it got difficult with time. You started drinking beer; suddenly studies became more important to you. You had begun to avoid me. I never thought the man of my dreams would behave like this. I never thought my Mr Perfect would ignore me. The same man who once sang songs for me, who had gone on his knees and proposed to me, had now begun to avoid me.'

'Slowly, everything began to fade around me. I had never thought of making good friends in college since I loved your company and that was enough for me. When you suddenly went away from me, I was left all alone in college. I did not have anyone to share my feelings with. I could have told Swapnil and Anup but I did not as I did not want to hurt your friendship with them. But by doing this, I had become more lonely. You never realized all this. Earlier you used to understand every small need of mine but how could you ignore what I felt? How?'

'It started from the day you ignored my calls. Remember? More than 20 calls I think. Right? I was awake the whole night. I wanted to talk to you. I wanted to tell you so many things. I called Amit to ask what was wrong with you. His phone was busy. I guess he was talking with Neha. He called me after an hour or so. I told him about you. I told him about our problems so that he could make you understand.'

While she told me this, I kept thinking to myself how she could have talked about her problems with Neha. She could have expressed her feelings to Swapnil. I didn't understand how it would have hurt our friendship. Maybe she just wanted excuses. I said sorry for whatever I did that night. I said I was tired. Even I am human. She could have understood. 'I love you jaan. I love you. Why did you do this?'

She continued, 'I told Amit about the problems in our relationship. He said, "What are you saying! I never thought Aditya could behave like this. He seemed perfect. What happened to him? He loves you so much. Every time we talk, we talk only about you. He is a darling. I can't believe he is behaving like this."'

Bloody rascal. If he thought I was perfect, why was he dating my jaan? People had always taken advantage of her sweetness. Now it was Amit.

Riya continued, 'I had called up Amit and said, "Amit, just think what might be running through my mind. I never gave him any chance to complain. I gave him whatever he wanted. I gave him such lovely presents on his birthday and still he is behaving like I don't matter to him. I called him so many times. Please can you call him and ask?" This is the reason he called you that day. Even Neha called you that day. But you still didn't bother. You wanted your sleep.'

'Amit called me again that night and said, "Aditya is not picking up the call. He might be sleeping. He might be tired today. Don't think over it too much. This must be new to you. I am used to this. Neha always does this to me. I wait outside the college for hours and she never bunks lectures. I want to meet her but she never meets me. I am used to this type of behaviour." I cried. I was crying a lot. He consoled me saying he would talk to you. He did talk to you. Still you never heard him. You had changed Aadi... I had lost my old Aditya. He died. He died the day our exams ended.'

I knew this bastard would tell Riya about his problems with Neha. There was no need to tell her that he was used to it. What the hell did he mean? Why did he want to persuade Riya? 'I never did anything on purpose. It's not that I had stopped loving you, Riya. I wanted to give you all happiness in the future. I wanted to study for you. So that my mom would accept you from her heart. You couldn't understand something as simple as this? Why bachcha? Why?'

But Riya's complaints were not over. She continued with her explanation, 'Your behaviour became worse day by day. I thought you had stopped loving me. I thought you never loved me. Did you? Why did you change so suddenly? The day you said you wanted a breakup, I almost lost my senses. I had never expected to hear this. We loved each other so much that I never thought you would betray me. I was really upset. I was broken completely. I was in pain, I was frustrated, and all I could think about was you and your love.'

'What could I do? How could I save a broken relationship? Breaking up is a terrible, painful experience, no doubt, especially if you feel that you have lost the love of your life. Amit was with me in those days. He supported me when I needed someone whom I could rely on, whom I could tell how I was feeling. I tried contacting you. I tried messaging you. You never responded to any of my calls.'

When she knew how it felt after a break up, why did she do the same thing to me? Was she taking revenge? When she knew how much pain it caused, why did she do the same to me? She felt that love of her life is lost? However, I felt like I had lost my life itself. 'Please come back, jaan. Please come back. I need you. I am still your Aditya.'

Riya hadn't finished. 'One of those days, Amit asked me to go on a bike ride with him. A long ride on his bike. I refused at first as I didn't want to hurt you. When he asked me for the ride, I tried calling you. You messaged me not to disturb you. You wanted your studies. I was really upset that day. The next day Amit again asked me for a ride. I didn't get any reply from you. So I accepted his offer. I wanted someone to share my feelings with. I thought spending some time with him would change my mood and help me brighten my mood. I met him at the depot. He was waiting for me with his bike. He had brought chocolates for me. It brought a smile on my face. I sat on his bike and we headed towards Palm Beach Road.'

If anyone wanted to know how to take advantage of the sweetest girl in town, if any one wanted to know how to use the emotions of a girl, he should contact

Amit. He never once thought about Neha before asking her for a ride. What about her love? Did she mean nothing to him? What was happening? Why was Amit doing this? I wanted to hit him straight on his dick! How could he do this?

'He was driving too fast. I avoided holding him but I had to as he was driving fast. I got hold of him by his waist. It brought tears ito my eyes. It was the first time I had touched someone other than you after you had come in my life. I was feeling awkward. I told him to slow down. He did. I removed my hand from his waist. He made me smile, he made me laugh. After an hour or so, we left for Sea Woods.'

This is unreal. This can't be happening to me. I wanted to pinch myself to believe whether it was a bad dream or something so I could wake up and it would all be over. But I knew it was all too real. My girlfriend went on a long drive with another guy! What could be worse than that? The worst part was that bloody guy was my friend. How could Riya do this to me? How could Amit allow Riya to do this?

'As we reached Grant Lane, I said "Where are we going Amit? It's late." He told me "I wanted to tell you something about Neha. Let's go to that garden. We will leave in half an hour. Is it fine?" I told him it wasn't a problem. But we will have to leave early. Otherwise you would have shouted at me. By the time we reached the garden, it was already dark. We sat on a bench in one corner. He bought ice cream for me. As we were having the ice cream, he said, "Riya, I am not happy. I am not getting what I want. I am giving my best to our relationship but still I'm not happy." I asked him what happened and if there was any problem or conflicts with Neha.'

'He replied saying, "Yes. She does not give any respect to me. I wait for her bunking my college and she doesn't care. She keeps making silly excuses. I call her in the break when she is with her friends. I really admire your relationship with Aditya."'

'I told him, "What admire? Can't you see how Aditya is behaving with me? All charm in our relationship is gone." He said "I always wanted a girl who would care for me, who would look after my little needs, who would understand my feelings and would love me more than anyone else in this world. When I will be with her, I will forget what is going around me. When she will hold my hand, I would feel like I have achieved everything in life. When I will kiss her, I would feel she is the only one I wanted. I wanted a girl like this."'

'I tried to convince him and said, "I really don't see any good qualities in Neha. She is a very different kind of girl. Her priorities are different. Her life is different. I wanted a girl who would be with me for a lifetime, someone who would give me priority. During our schooldays, I thought Neha would be the girl who would fit this bill. But as it turns out, I was wrong. Today I think I took a wrong decision. The day I saw you, I instantly liked you. You were a changed girl. Anyone could fall for you at first sight. But I ignored you since I felt I loved Neha and she deserved another chance. But day by day, we came closer. We started talking during nights for hours. I really felt you were the girl I could trust. I didn't know what was happening. I should not do this. I should ignore the temptation. I should have kept myself calm. I should have stopped my heart from falling for you. But I really could not. If you don't like what I'm telling you, please tell me to stop and I will not repeat it again, I promise. Nevertheless, for now I want you. I want to feel you. I want to feel what was in you that was forcing me to do what I am going to do. I want to feel your lips." said Amit staring at me.'

Oh gosh! This was the extreme. If he had been standing in front of me, I would have killed him. How could he have done this? Our friendship meant nothing to him. The girl he wants to kiss means nothing to me? My feelings, my love—all of it were inconsequential for him. I had heard people change with time. But change to such extent? Is Riya really so innocent that she gave in to his promises so easily? Riya wake up! Open your eyes and see that this guy is fooling you. He just wants to get you into bed with him. Please jaan, wake up before it's too late.

Riya continued with her explanation and said, 'I was shocked to hear about his feelings for me. Before I could react, he came closer and touched my lips. Before I could tell him that it was wrong, he felt my lips. Before I could tell him that I was committed to you, I felt his saliva in my mouth. Before I could tell him what we were going to do was wrong, he kissed me passionately. Before I could feel anything about you, he closed my eyes. Before I could stop myself, he was kissing me so passionately that I could not stop him. Rather, I could not stop my self from kissing him back. I still don't know it was right or wrong. But I can still feel that moment. The way he looked in my eyes, I saw the same love that was in your eyes. Before I could resist, he went on kissing me...'

I felt as if a thousand daggers had stabbed me in the heart. I had been shattered into pieces. Riya kissed him. Who of all the people? My so called 'good friend' Amit. My friend Amit kissed who? My sweetheart Riya? What was I doing? I was bloody listening to whatever happened like a fool. Did she enjoy it?

'I stopped him finally. We did not speak a word after the kiss. Both of us had tears in our eyes. Both of us cried. We came closer. We kissed again. We hugged. All our pent-up frustration was releasing. I never wanted this to happen. I wanted you. I wanted my Aditya. My Mr Perfect. However, destiny had something else in store for me.'

Now what was the use of saying she never wanted this to happen? It was real. Not a dream. Not a nightmare. She had kissed him. She had kissed my friend in the same garden where we had celeberated my birthday.

Did I mean nothing to her?

'We returned. We didn't speak a single word. He left me near my house. I went home. I slept on my bed. I could not control my tears. I did not know why I was crying. In the last few days, I had cried for you. But today I was confused. Was it for you who betrayed me or was it because of Amit who had made me smile…?'

'I still did not know why the tears came. But I loved you. I loved you like crazy and you can't deny that fact. The entire college knew this.'

He was wrong, very wrong. I was disappointed with him. He should not have taken advantage of my girlfriend. He should not have crossed the line. It was impossible to forgive him now.

If the heart was the most important organ, then why did it break so easily? I would still forgive her. But Amit had made so much impact on her that she just ignored my love. She had forgotten everything.

Pyaar mein ashk behate kyun hain…
Do dil ek doosre ko tadpaate kyun hain…
Kehte hain pyaar zindagi hai…
Toh phir pyaar ko khel banaate kyun hain…

Riya's Confession Continues

'I was guilty. I wanted to tell you whatever had happened. I wanted to confess in front of you that I had kissed Amit. I never wanted to go away from you. If I had told you about the kiss, the distance between us would have increased. I didn't want to lose you. Your one decision changed our lives.'

'I decided not to go anywhere. It would have further brought him closer to me. I did not want to hurt Neha. She was my only good friend in college. I decided not to talk to him often. I started avoiding him, even though he was the only one after you who had made me smile.'

'I could not forget our first kiss. I could not forget the feel of it. Why did you take the decision of going away from me? One decision of yours changed everything, jaan. I never wanted this to happen. I wanted to marry you. But you changed everything.'

'Amit called me the next day. He wanted to meet me. He said, "Please forget whatever happened yesterday. I know you love Aadi. I know you can never be mine. But can we meet as friends? I want to see you." I told him, "No Amit. I can't. After whatever happened yesterday I can't meet you. I don't want to encourage you and be the reason for your breakup with Neha. Please. I am sorry."'

'I was confused. Why did I refuse to meet him? I should say I didn't want to encourage myself. I was really frustrated and wanted to leave all the things behind. I wanted to forget you... But I thought it was bringing me closer to Amit.'

'That night you called me. I was overwhelmed when I heard your voice. I was in tears. I could not stop them. You sang our favorite song: *Tujhe dekh dekh sona...*'

'It made me cry even more. I could not say anything. I realized then that you were my true love. I realized that no one could replace you. I loved you jaan. I loved you a lot. I was excited to talk to you the next morning in class. I thought we could spend an entire day together. But you were leaving for Ratnagiri. I was upset after hearing this. I went home. I was checking my mailbox. God knows what came to my mind and I checked your mailbox too. I saw a mail in your draft. A girl named Muskaan had e-mailed you. It had been sent on September 16. It said:

"Hi sweetie. I am missing you. I enjoyed every moment with you. You can make any girl feel special. Your body looks so hot when you are wet. I love you. I love your back. I can never forget the time we had a bath together. My bed is missing you. I want you right now on my bed. Please come back to my home. I am waiting."'

'I could not believe what I was looking at. You had never told me about Muskaan and that you had slept with her. You even had a bath with her! My blood pressure turned low. Doctors told me to take rest. I was shattered. I wanted someone with whom I could share all these things. But there was no one. I was all alone. I could have accepted you if you had told me this from the very beginning. But you didn't. You lied to me. You had told me once that you had not been physical with any girl. You lied. I could never trust you. Things were getting worse between us. I loved you a lot. I was always so frank with you. Still you lied to me. It was a shock for me. I called Swapnil to ask him who Muskaan was. He told me everything about her. He told me every small thing he knew about you and Muskaan. He told me Muskaan was your girlfriend and that you were very close with her. She was from Delhi. She was your friend's friend. He even told me he had asked you to tell me everything. But you didn't.'

'I could not forget what he told me. Muskaan was your girlfriend. This was the cheapest e-mail I had ever read and you are the cheapest guy too. You broke all the promises you had made to me. Each promise was broken:

1. We will always be together… You left me alone.
2. We will never fight…. You broke up with me.
3. Our love will never fade…. You cheated on me.
4. Trust…. I can't trust you anymore.
5. Respect for each other… You never understood my feelings.
6. Forget each other's past… Now I understand why this promise was taken.
7. Good education… I never cared about it when I was with you.'

'You broke all the promises, jaan. You broke my life into pieces. Some things happen even if we don't want them to. And we have to accept them. Even I had to accept that you had changed. You were not my Aadi. You had changed a lot. You had created your own world. I was depressed. I wanted someone with whom I could share all these things. I could not control myself. I called Amit. I told him everything that I had seen. He asked me to meet him in Aerol. I went to meet him.'

'He made me smile even in those difficult moments. I was getting attracted towards him. He tried to kiss me. But I didn't allow him to. I was depressed. I wanted to be alone. This was the reason why I didn't answer you when you left for Ratnagiri. I wanted to go away from you. I could never trust you. I called you so many times. But your phone was out of coverage area. You must have kept it in the offline mode on purpose.'

'The next day Amit messaged me. He asked me to go on a date with him to south Mumbai. I agreed to go with him. I was waiting for him at the bus stop. He came with his bike. We left. We went to McDonald's in south Mumbai. We enjoyed ourselves the entire day. After a long time I was laughing and having a good time. We went to Reclamations, Carter Road. It was good fun.'

'It was 5 pm by the time we decided to return. Amit was driving his bike slowly. He was looking at me continuously in the rear view mirror. Even I was looking at him. I was holding on to him tightly from behind. Suddenly he put his hand on mine and his touch sent a shiver down my spine. We reached Aerol. I thanked him for the lovely day.'

'He asked me, "Is it urgent for you to go home?"' I said "No. Nothing like that. I have time. Why?"'

'He answered, 'We can go to my place. There is no one at home. Only if it's fine with you." I was confused. I was afraid to go to his home. Still I took up the offer. We went to his house. It was a small house with just one room. I sat on the sofa. He went inside the kitchen to make tea for me. A few minutes later, he came out with tea and bisucits on a tray. He placed the tray on the table and came and sat next to me. He moved closer to me, but I moved away from him.'

'He complimented me on my looks and said, "You are looking so hot today, Riya. You are beautiful. You understand me so well." We were both looking into each other's eyes. I wanted to break all the barriers and go with him. I had started liking him. He sensed that. He squeezed my thighs and we kissed each other. We did much more than a kiss. We went all the way that day. I still don't know if it was for revenge or I had started loving him. Maybe it was a mixture of both. I went home. Amit messaged me.:

I wanted a girl like you. I always wished for a girlfriend like you. Can we be together? I love you. Listen to your heart. Don't worry about the world. I am ready to face the entire world if you are by my side. Don't think about what people say. Think and answer... I will wait.

'I tried calling you again. But I got the same response. You must have been busy sleeping with someone. I thought about Amit's proposal. And we came close and today we are together.'

I was speechless. I could not speak a word. I had lost myself. I had lost everything. Still after hearing this why did my heart still love her. I wanted her back. I was ready to forgive her for whatever she had done in the last 5 days. All I could think of was what she had done for me in the last one year and not in the last 5 days. I wanted her badly. Jaan I love you. Please come back jaan. Please come back. I love you a lot.

I wanted my Riya back.

Mistakes

So it was true. Riya was out of my life. Why did it have to end like this? I don't understand how you could do this to me. I really didn't deserve this. Just one more chance was all I asked for. Suddenly there were tears running down my face. And nothing could stop them from falling, you had left without saying a single word.

I wondered why I had taken that decision of leaving her for a few days. Those days changed my life forever.

I told Neha about what had happened. She was in a state of utter shock. She told me Amit was ignoring her completely. Seeing her so upset brought tears to my eyes too.

'How can Amit do something like this?' I cried. 'That man is a bastard. Tell him to fuck off.' I was angry.

'Please Aadi. Stop saying this. I will make him understand.'

'There is no use making him understand now. They have gone too far in their relationship. But still I want my Riya back. He has just made a fool out of her.'

'What do you mean by saying they have gone too far in their relationship? Are you insane? What are you saying!' she cried.

'They were together the entire day and then went back to his place together.' She didn't want to hear any further and kept the phone down.

I knew how it felt hearing something like this about your love.

She called me back again after a few hours.

'Can you come to Aerol? I will talk to Amit. We will meet him. Please come. I can't live like this anymore.' She sounded depressed.

I agreed to come. Even I wanted to talk to Amit. I had so many unanswered questions ready for him in my mind. I told Neha to call him while I was on the way. I told her to keep the call on conference. I wanted to hear what they were saying. I wanted to hear what was on his mind. She agreed to do as I said.

I took my Activa and left for Aerol. I tuned on my radio. Neha called me. 'Have you left?'

I told her to call him up and not to tell him about the conference call. I told her to say that she was travelling and if any kind of disturbance was coming then that was because she was on the streets. She called Amit and put me on conference without telling him.

Amit: 'Why have you called? I am busy. Call me later.'

Neha: 'Please Amit. I want to talk to you. Aditya told me everything that is going on between you and Riya. Why did you do this?'

Amit: 'I didn't do anything. Got it. You deserve it. You didn't give anything that I wanted. Riya is keeping me happy. She is a darling.'

Neha: 'I loved you so much. Aditya loves Riya so much. Why did you have to propose to her?'

Amit: 'Please don't tell me that you loved me. You never loved me. As for Aditya, I don't care about him. He could not handle a darling sweet girl like Riya. Now she is mine.'

I did not want to hear all this. But I had to. I wanted to know what was in his mind. I reached the Eastern Express highway. Their conversation continued.

Neha: 'What made you feel that way? I really loved you.'

Amit: 'You didn't. Forget about other things, you never even allowed me to kiss you. You never had trust in me. Leave it.'

Neha: 'So Riya is giving you everything. Does it mean she loves you? Where doess Aditya stand in this picture? Is he nothing for her?'

Amit: 'No, he is nothing. He is her past. I am her present and future. He has never been loyal to her. He slept with someone else and didn't tell her about it. This is not right.'

Neha: 'You are doing nothing different. You also didn't bother to tell me. You can never love anyone. I know it now.'

Amit: 'You don't have to teach me what is right and what is wrong. You want to hear the truth, then hear it. But you can never prove it.'

Neha: 'What do you want to say?'

Amit: 'I am with Riya because I want a physical relationship. I don't love her. And if she gives me what you didn't, then I can live with her for a long time. I will keep her happy.'

I had lost my senses by then. I knew he was fooling my Riya. But who was going to make Riya understand? I was losing my mind.

Neha: 'You are a bastard. Why are you doing this? I love you Amit. I can't live without you. Please Amit please. Please come back to me. I will give you whatever you want. But please don't leave me.'

Amit: 'Sorry, now I won't. She is so hot. Much more hotter than you. You get lost now. I will give her what Aditya could not give.'

I interrupted their conversation. I could not control myself.

Me: 'Madarchod, don't you feel any guilt? You are talking about your friend's girlfriend.'

Amit: 'Aditya, have you been listening to our conversation all this while? I will kill you Neha. Aditya, just leave Riya and me alone. She is my girlfriend now. You could not give her the pleasure that I can.'

Me: 'You bastard! Some relationships mean more than sex. And you are fooling Riya! You used her vulnerability to your advantage while I was gone. I had never thought you could do something like this.'

Amit: 'Bloody loser. You slept with someone else and are now telling me to stop doing so. I will sleep with her.'

I was driving my bike at full speed. I wanted to reach Aerol as soon as possible. I wanted to tell Riya that this man was fooling her. I wanted to stop Riya from going any further with him. She was too sweet and innocent to know that she was being taken advantage of. She must be thinking Amit loved her. But he just wanted her in his bed.

Amit: 'And one more thing, Aditya. The black spot on her back is really sexy. It feels so good to kiss her there.'

I could not control myself. I wanted to hit him hard. I was so angry that I didn't see a bus coming at full speed in my direction. By the time I realized I was too close to the bus, it was too late. I tried to apply the brakes but I lost control over my bike.

The next thing I remember is that there was a huge crowd surrounding me. My legs and hands were bleeding. My entire body was aching badly. But the injuries did not look so serious. My headset was lost. People around me gave me water and I was alright in few minutes. I somehow sat on my Activa again and started driving. I wanted to meet all of them as quickly as possible. My injuries didn't hurt as much as my heart did. I reached Aerol.

Riya saw me bleeding from a distance. She was with Neha and Amit. She came running towards me. I was parking my Activa. She started crying looking at my condition. She asked me what had happened and shouted at me saying that I always was a rash driver. For one minute I thought my Riya was back, like she hadn't forgotten me completely. But she regained her composure soon. I felt like she still loved me. But was afraid. She loved Amit too. Maybe she didn't love me anymore. I didn't know what to believe anymore.

All our relationships had undergone a sea change—Amit was not a friend anymore. Riya was not my girlfriend anymore. Neha was not Amit's girlfriend anymore. Neha and Riya were no longer friends.

Seeing that we wanted a bit of time to talk it out with each other, Neha and Amit went and stood at a distance. I was with Riya. She didn't even look into my eyes.

'What happened, bachcha? Did I hurt you so much that you left me and accepted Amit in a wink?'

She didn't say anything. She had tears in her eyes.

'Jaan please don't cry. I still love you in the same way as I used to. Please say something jaan. Was I not worthy of your love?'

'It's not like that Aadi. But you took me for granted. I loved you even more than my life. But our relationship was getting worse. There was no point in being together,' she said.

'I love you jaan. I can't live without you now. Even my parents know about you. Please don't behave like this. I will change. Give me one more chance. I promise to prove you wrong,' I almost cried.

'You can never be my Aadi again.' She took my hand in hers to see how much blood was oozing. She wiped it off with her napkin.

'You forgot everything that happened between us? The 7 promises, my birthday, everything? You really don't love me anymore?' I was looking into her eyes.

'Aadi, I care for you. I can't see you like this. Please be normal and happy. I want you to smile.'

'Great. How can I smile when you are with someone else? You were the smile on my face. I will miss all those memories. Please come back. Please,' I pleaded.

'I can't, Aadi. I can't. I can never trust you. I can't break Amit's trust now. But I want you to smile. I want you to take care of yourself. I want you to eat properly. Don't misbehave with your mom. Study well. Please try to forget me. I am not saying I won't talk to you again. But please don't make me cry by making a sad face. I can't see my sweet little bachcha crying. I want him to enjoy his life even without me. You will always be special to me. Please forgive me.

Take care. I will always miss you till my dying breath,' she cried.

'How can I do all these things without you jaan? Please come back. I can't handle this. I don't want to. Give me one chance. Please.'

She was walking away from me. My heart was bleeding. I was watching my love going away from me and I could do nothing about it. Nothing at all. This made me more depressed. I wanted her. I could not handle my life without her. I was used to being with her. I loved her.

Neha was also crying. Even Amit was firm on his decision to break up with Neha. I wanted to tell Riya about Amit's real intentions. But I didn't because it would have made the situation worse. She was totally under his influence. She would never have listened to me at that moment. Amit smiled at me. He caught Riya's hand and went away.

'Aadi, please stop them. Please. I can't see them together. I can't face this,' Neha cried.

I did not say anything. My heart was bleeding.

Now I was beginning to understand what someone had once said—some love stories can never be predicted.

All Alone

I could never forget the days we spent together. We had a lot of fun, especially when we were together. I will always remember her presence in college. The laughter that we shared, the dreams that we had, and the promises we made. But those dreams changed with time and left a big hole in my heart. I knew she had moved on in her life. She had got someone better than me. But I still wished she cared for me.

I was all alone in college. I missed her everywhere. I stopped going to the canteen. Whenever I went there, I could see that table where we used to sit. Where we sang songs together. I stopped listening to our favourite song because it made me cry even more. It became difficult for me to face others. I wanted to avoid everyone. Having lunch all alone made me love her even more. I could see her in college. Though she talked to me occasionally, she was not the same Riya anymore.

I had to attend lectures as PL, the official study leave before exams, was hardly a week away. Everything seemed to be different. I was missing her badly. I was regretting my decision. In fact I had started loving her more than before. I realized love had no limits. I realized what I had heard was actually true. Break up always made you love your girlfriend more. I was facing the same thing. Swapnil, Sameer, and Anup came to see me. I had been ignoring them for the last few days. I was not in the mood to face the world. They landed up at home one day and asked me what was the problem.

'Riya broke up with me. She left me all alone. I think I don't deserve her. But I still love her. I love her very much. I want her back in my life.'

'What happened? Why did she leave you? You must have done something wrong. Don't worry, she will come back to you eventually,' Swapnil said.

'She won't come back to me. She has a new boyfriend now,' I said with tears rolling down my face.

'Are you silly? What are you saying? She can't do this. She loves you so much. You both love each other. You are a perfect couple. So stop saying negative things,' Sameer said.

'I am serious. I know it. She is with Amit now. I hope you remember him.'

'What are you saying? I can't believe this. But how? Why? What about Neha? Shall I talk to her? 'Swapnil seemed surprised.

I didn't answer them. I just went away. I was upset. I was fed up with all these questions. I went to class.

She was not with me. She was sitting on some other bench. I felt frustrated.

After the class was over, she talked with me for a few minutes about frivolous things that had no meaning. But she got a call in the middle of our conversation and left. I was alone again. The feeling of loneliness was killing me. I wanted to talk to her.

I messaged her: `Can we talk tonight? I am missing you. Please jaan.`

She replied saying, `Okay. Call me at 11 pm.`

There were no sweet words in the message. I was waiting for the clock to strike 11. I was eager to talk to her.

I called her at 11 sharp.

But I got an automated response from the network provider saying ,'The number you are trying to call is busy.' I tried again but got the same response. I called Amit. Even his phone was busy. I knew she was talking to him. I called up Neha. She told me that she had been trying Amit's number since the past few minutes.

'Aadi, it's all over. I don't think Amit will come back to me. He doesn't even reply to my messages now. Riya at least replies to yours. He is avoiding me completely. I am broken. Please do something.'

'What can I do? I am sailing in the same boat. Even I want my Riya back. Even I want to feel her love. But I am helpless. I am trying my level best to bring her back. I am going to ask her to come with me tomorrow,' I said.

'Do you think she will come with you? I don't think so. They have forgotten us,' she replied dejectedly.

'Please don't say this. I won't let her go so easily.' I called her once again. Again her cell was busy. I sent her a message saying I needed to talk to her urgently.

She didn't reply.

I waited for her call till 3 am. Waiting for so long made me realize what she must have felt when I ignored her calls that day. I was crying. Her busy ringtone was killing me. Finally she called me back.

'What is so urgent that you keep calling me again and again? Don't you understand I was on call with someone? Now say what you want to say.' She seemed angry.

'Jaan, I was missing you. I want to meet you. I really love you jaan. Please forgive me. Please come back,' I cried.

'Is this what you wanted to tell me? Is it so urgent?'

'No. I wanted to ask you if tomorrow we could go out somewhere for the whole day—just the two of us?' I knew she would not agree to it.

'No. I have work tomorrow at home. I can come day after tomorrow.'

As she said this I smiled.

'Ok jaan. No problem. I will be waiting for day after tomorrow.' I saw the date on the calendar. This could not be a miracle. She had planned the meeting on October 11—her birthday. I really thought God had a role to play in it. I messaged her: Your birthday will be special. Full of surprises...miss you.

Changing Relationships

It was October 11—her birthday. I wanted to make her realize what she meant to me. I wanted to make her realize that no one could love her more than me. I wanted to relive the moments of my birthday. With the same surprises and a few more. I knew if today I could make her realize how much I loved her, she would never go back to Amit.

We had decided to go to Chowpatty. I could have taken her to Grant Lane but I was afraid because she had been with Amit to Grant Lane only a few days back. We boarded the train. I took out the first surprise from my bag.

' A white rose to clear the fights between us,' I said handing over the rose to her.

She accepted it. But there was no reaction on her face.

'Thanks but…' I stopped her from saying anything else.

Maybe I knew what she was going to say. She was not the same Riya. She was looking out of the window and I was looking at her. I took out the second rose for her after some time.

'A yellow rose for our friendship. A friendship that we once shared. We can still go back to that,' I said.

'I don' think we can be what we were. Time changes everything. Still thanks again,' she said and gave me a weak smile.

I was losing my temper. But I didn't want to fight. I kept cool. We got out of the station and called for an autorickshaw. I took out the third surprise for her. It was a letter. I had written it personally for her.

I remember the day we met for the first time. I was in love the moment I saw you. Slowly both of us came together. I loved the way you took care of me. I loved the way you called me bachcha. I loved the way you smiled at me. I loved the way you kissed me. I loved the way you looked at me. There is nothing in you which I hate. Nothing at all. If there is something that I hate, it's my fault. You could never be wrong. I love you more than myself. I am sorry. I am sorry and I am really sorry. I want to live those moments again with you. I want to propose to you again.

I can't forget whatever you did for me in the last one year. But I'm ready to forget whatever you did with me in the last few days. Please jaan, can we be the same Aditya and Riya who used to be the famous couple in our colony, in our college, and among our friends? Can we be together again? I am ready to accept all your faults and change all my faults. But please don't go away. I can't see you with anyone else. Love you a lot.

Your Aditya

She kept the letter with her. I was happy to see tears in her eyes. It meant she still had some feelings for me and everything was not over yet. I tried to hold her hand. She didn't allow me to. I was upset by her reaction. Still I smiled at her. I was pampering her continuously, trying to make her smile and enjoy each moment.

'Jaan, are you happy with whatever decision you have taken? Do you really think Amit can keep you happy? Do you feel he loves you?' I asked her.

'Yes, he loves me. He really does. And please let's not talk about that,' she said irritatedly.

'How can you say he loves you? If he can betray Neha, he can betray you too,' I said.

'I don't care what he did with Neha. Now he is with me and we love each other. I am with you because I care for you. Nothing else. So please don't call me by nick names. I am in a relationship. It doesn't look good.'

This was too much. Now I cannot call my Riya by her pet name also. She used to call me bachcha. Now what? Everything I was doing was going wrong. We reached Chowpatty.

We were sitting on the seashore looking at the waves. I was making her recollect all those moments that we spent together. She had tears in her eyes. I gave her another surprise. It was another letter.

I want today to be special. I want your birthday to be celebrated the same way we had celebrated mine. These few days have been the worst days of my life. Still today I want you and me together. I want to give you smile and tears. I want you to feel me.

I knew something was wrong from day one. But I didn't say a word. When you told me you went on a bike ride with him, I should have told you it was wrong. When you told me you and he slept together, I should have asked how could you? But I didn't say a word. How could I sit back and watch your world be destroyed?

He is playing with you. But you won't understand this now.

That burning desire to touch your skin won't go away. Maybe you will just kiss me again, and pretend you like me and want me again. But I don't want you to pretend. All I want is that you should wake up from the dreamworld he is showing you before it's too late. Or there is one option. Would that be better for you?

I can pretend that I don't cry for you the whole day. We can pretend we never loved each other and we both used each other for physical needs. In reality there will always be that throbbing pain in our hearts.

We can pretend that you were nothing in my life. We can also pretend every small promise was fake.

Is this a good option for you? Another option is we can stop pretending and come back together because we know we neither used each other nor did we want each other for physical needs. We loved each other like crazy. We cared for each other like crazy. Please think it over again jaan. I want you to be my Riya. My mom wants you to be mine. When everybody is with us, why do you want to go against the world? To just fall down from a cliff? There is only death after that. Trust me.

She cried after reading this. I pulled her close to me. She rested her head on my shoulders. I thought I had got my Riya back. But she regained composure and apologized for having done that. I was helpless. I could not do anything.

We had so much love and passion for each other. But now it was all gone. We had made so many promises which were all lies.

It hurt to hear that she was in another relationship. I knew our relationship was progressing too quickly. It was only when we went away from each other did I realise what she meant to me. I really wonder now if she would ever call me 'my sweet little bachcha' again.

We were walking on the beach. The sun was about to set. I took her near the water and told her to look at the sun. We both removed our shoes and I told her to stand on my feet.

'It's so far. Still we can see it so clearly. It's such a romantic sky, all orange, still we can't feel the romance.

I want you to close your eyes. I want you to feel we are in each others arms,' I said

She closed her eyes.

'We are hugging each other on the sea shore. We are married. We are living a happy life. I ask you how many children you want. You are smiling like a new bride. I can see the naughtiness in your eyes. Tell me Riya. How many children do you want?'

She didn't answer. She was quiet. She opened her eyes and turned towards me. She had tears in her eyes. Even I had tears in my eyes. I knew she was imagining the 7 promises that we had made to each other.

She hugged me. She was the same Riya who never thought of what people around us were thinking about our PDA.

'Why Aadi…? Why did you take that decision. It still hurts. It still hurts badly. Now I can't do anything. When I loved you more than my life, you didn't care. Now when I am with someone else, you say you love me more than anything else. It's too late Aadi. I can't come back now. I just care for you. You are still my bachcha. But I can't come back now and be with you,' she said.

'Why jaan? We can still be together. Amit does not love you. He is with you just because he wants you to go to bed with him. He told me all this himself. Please jaan, realize the gravity of the situation before it's too late. I still love you. I am ready to accept you as you are. But I can't let you go. Come back Riya. Please.

I went on my knees with a red rose. Everyone around was watching us with weird expressions on their faces.

I ignored them all.

'I love you. I still love you the way I used to when we had first met. I can still sing the same song. But today I want to sing something different. Just two lines:

Rooth ke hamse kabhi jab chale jaaoge tum...

Yeh na socha tha kabhi...

Itne yaad aaoge tum...

Please jaan. I am sorry. Will you marry me?'

She was crying. But she didn't react. She didn't accept my rose. She started walking away. I was still on my knees. I was watching her go. I got up and went towards her. I tried to convince her. But she didn't agree. There was silence in the auto too while we returned back home.

I gave her the final letter of the day.

The sweet memories are fading. It is getting harder to remember the last time you smiled for me. Those memories of love are fading. Your smiling face is becoming blurred in my mind. So you really don't love me anymore? Or is it something else that is stopping you?

Your words are fading into silence. I can't remember the last time we kissed. It's been so long.

Please understand I'm not forgetting on purpose, it hurts me not to remember. But it feels like it has been decades since the last time we made love. Please don't cry while reading this. Please bachcha stop crying. If there is nothing in your heart for me what are these tears for? You should stop them too.

Would you forgive me if I told you that I can't remember the day you said you love me? It's not my mistake this time. I seriously don't remember the last time you had played with my hair. The last time you played with my eyes. The last time you held my hands tightly. The last time you were so close to me that we seemed one. The last time when you sang a song for me. Today it hurts when I think of all those things. Today I have deleted that song from my memory. It only hurts. Please tell me what is stopping you? Is everything really over or is it a nightmare? All I know and all I can feel is that these sweet memories are fading away.

And so are you.

She hugged me. We were both crying. I realized she couldn't be mine. I could feel that from her touch. Something was missing. In fact everything was missing. Was it my mistake or was it hers? All I knew was she was getting trapped into it by Amit. I was helpless. I could have hit him. But I didn't want to. It would have increased the distance between Riya and me.

Times had changed. Relationships had changed. Love had disappeared.

We reached home. I called Swapnil, Sameer, and Anup. I told them whatever had happened. They agreed to convince Riya to come back.

Break Up

This was my last chance. If I could not get her now, I would have to forget her forever—something I didn't want to. I requested all my friends to brainwash her against Amit. I could not see her falling into his trap. We decided to meet in Aerol. I was scared about the outcome of this meeting. I felt like my life was moving towards a dead end. I was thinking about all the possibilities.

We were all waiting for Riya near the college. We had planned to meet Neha too. When Riya came, she completely ignored me. She didn't even look at me. She was talking to Swapnil. We went to a restaurant. I didn't order anything. I was tensed. Swapnil initiated the conversation.

'What happened Riya? Why you have changed suddenly? Has Aditya been troubling you? You can be frank with us and tell us everything.'

'I did not change suddenly. It took me a long time to take this decision. Your friend Aditya changed suddenly. You can ask him. I don't need to say anything,' said Riya and looked at me.

'I know Aditya changed. He took a wrong decision. I slapped him for that. But he has realized his mistake. You both loved each other so much. Can't you forgive him?' Swapnil said.

'Look Riya, somewhere along the way everyone makes a mistake. Even Aditya did. But it doesn't mean you will go to someone else. We know how Amit is in real life, Sameer added while Anup nodded his head in agreement.

'I don't know who is speaking the truth here. All I know is that I have had a chance to know Amit personally for a few days. I know him personally. He really loved Neha but Neha didn't care for him at all. I don't say I never loved Aditya. I cared for him like a mother. I treated him like my child. But he took me for granted. He started avoiding me. I could have tolerated that. But what about Muskaan? He never told me about her. He just told me about his girlfriend. Nothing else. Why did he have to lie to me?' Riya said.

'I didn't lie to you. I didn't want to hurt you. If I was playing with you, then why I would keep that mail. Just think, Muskaan wanted to spoil my name.' I said almost crying.

'I don't know anything Aditya, but now it's not possible to be together. Please forget me,' she said angrily.

Swapnil took her outside. I was tensed. Sameer and Anup calmed me down. I was worried as to what was going to happen. They came inside after a few minutes. Swapnil paid the bill and was about to leave.

' Swapnil, what is happening? Please can you tell me. Please. Did she agree?' I asked him curiously.

'It's all over, Aditya. Now she won't listen. You will have to pay for your one decision. She doesn't love you anymore. Get on with your life. At least be happy that she is talking to you.'

I did not say anyting. Riya left. Sameer called Neha to come near the bus depot.

Once there, Sameer asked her, 'What have you decided? Aadi can't let her go. He wants her back after knowing everything. What is your decision?'

She smiled.

'Nothing. I don't expect anything. I don't know about Riya. But Amit wouldn't come back for sure. He wouldn't talk to me. I don't want to get into all this. Exams are coming. Seriously I don't care about all this now. I am over it. Amit is a bastard and Riya is his bitch. Let them sleep or fuck. I don't care.'

I slapped Neha. I should not have done that. But I had to. I could not control myself after what she said.

'What are you saying? I am sorry to hit you. But you said something horrible. What do you mean by "let them fuck"? I will kill you and Amit both. You don't love him, I don't care. I love Riya and always will. I can't hear anything bad about her. Get lost.'

I was surprised by this side of Neha's nature. I had heard girls recover easily after break up. But it did not hold true for every girl. Neha was not one of them. She was over with the break up. Maybe she never loved him. Who cared? I loved Riya.

Without talking to anyone I left. It was all over. It was difficult to decide whether I should be happy that she was still in contact with me or upset that she had left me, breaking all the promises. I reached home. As I got down from my Activa, I saw I had got a message on my cell. It was Riya.

```
Swapnil tried to convince me. You should have
done something yourself. I know you tried. But
it was too late. Telling Swapnil to convince
me was the worst mistake you could have ever
made. If you could not handle a relationship,
why did you bring everyone else to do it for
you? I had told you my decision. I don't love
you. And from now onwards, I won't even talk
to you. I am changing my number today. So don't
try to contact me ever. Forget me. Take care
of yourself, and be serious about life. Miss
you always as a friend. Bye forever.
```

I called her immediately. She did not pick up. I messaged her. She did not reply. I called her several times but there was no response. I called Amit finally. He was not ready to speak to me.

'Amit, I don't want to talk to you. But can you please tell me what is wrong with Riya now? She messaged me that she didn't want to talk to me and she is changing her number. What is happening?'

'How could I know why she is changing her number? Maybe because she loves me a lot.' Amit laughed.

' What does that mean. Please care to explain,' I raised my voice.

'I told her to not to keep any contact with you. I told her not to message you or call you or even speak to you. She loves me too much. She accepted it and maybe that is the reason why she is changing her number. She is so sweet. And her black spot. I kissed her twice there.'

I kept the phone down. Everything was over. I could not hear what Amit was saying. I went upstairs to my bedroom.

I sent her a message communicating the end of everything.

It's okay. Forget me. Forget my memories. Forget the moments I spent with you. Forget the time I came to meet you without even thinking even once. Forget the promises that we made together. Forget my face. Forget my touch. Forget the time we kissed, loved each other or maybe I can say pretended to love each other. Forget my voice. Forget my craziness for you. Forget the conversations between us. Forget my family. Forget the day you come to my house. Forget the way I proposed to you.

Forget each day we spent together. Forget the
time we fought. Forget the time we patched
up.Forget my belongings with you. Throw it
away. Forget my name. Forget my number. Delete
it from your phone. Delete me from your life.
Forget me forever. This time forget seriously.
Goodbye. Stay happy with Amit. I will never
come in your way. Your chapter has been deleted
from my life forever. I will always love you.
I will always miss you. I will always keep your
gifts with me. I am yours and only yours. But
you were never mine.

Whatever the reason, it was enough for me to conclude
that breaking up was the only thing left. It was not easy
for me to send that message leaving behind everything,
but I had to. There was no other option left. I felt sad
for Riya. She was trapped. But I knew she would realize
it someday. I also knew she wouldn't ever be back. This
was the sad end. But if it had to be this way, I was ready
for it. At least I was ready to show I was okay with it.
But somewhere it hurt.

It was the end of everything.

The Worst Days of My Life

Exams came. I hadn't studied at all. I was going to screw up everything. I already had. I was making my life hell. I was not able to concentrate on anything. I had stopped listening to others. My mom was unaware of all these things. I did not want to hurt her. It was the end of life. I was just living for the sake of living. Exams came and went. I did not sit for two papers. I bunked two university papers of the third semester. Riya was in the same class as me. She was in the same examination hall. I left the hall and went away. I bunked Electrical Networks and Maths 2. I didn't care. The entire vacation was spent alone. I did not want to meet anyone. I lost contact with Neha. I didn't know where she was.

What was happening in her life? I lost contact with Riya. That hurt me the most. My heart still skipped a beat when I heard her name or saw her in college.

After 15 days, the exam results were displayed. I went all alone this time to see my result. I avoided Anup and

Swapnil. They were in IT and would get a chance to talk with Riya. Our group had broken. Everything had changed. Only Sameer was with me. My only friend.

I checked my result. It was not surprising. Three KTs.

Maths 2, Maths 3, and Electrical Networks…

I checked Riya's result. She had 2 KTs. I checked Neha's result. She had cleared. She never cared though. Everything changed. I didn't know what Amit's result was. He was in a different college. Neha was a closed chapter. Swapnil and Anup were no longer with me. Riya and Amit's story was a closed chapter for me. I had started screwing engineering. I had started screwing my life.

It was the beginning of the fourth semester. The day you left, I swore I'd never talk to you again. But that was just a wounded little boy in me talking. As I move on, I remembered all the times we had spent together. It was terrible facing the world without you. I could not concentrate in college. Each classroom made me feel like you were with me. Every moment was difficult to me. It was impossible to face college like this. It was like facing the sun when it's emitting the maximum sunlight. I tried to avoid every place in college where we had been together. But the funny thing was that there was none. We had left our mark on each and every hangout spot in the campus. Soon I started avoiding college itself. Each day I screwed up my life more and more.

'Aadi, please concentrate on your studies. You have a golden attempt paper and a KT also. At least attend all your lectures. Or else you will have problem during submissions,' Sameer said.

I couldn't face it. Whenever I went to college, I felt like crying. Whenever I saw her anywhere, I felt like talking to her. I had to admit that I couldn't get Riya back in my life but that made me love her even more. I told myself I should not be in the hope that she will ever come back to me. I was not supposed to wonder what Riya was doing and where she was, but I could not help it because I was in love with her. I seriously didn't know what was in her that made me behave like this.

When I saw her I just wanted her on the bed. As days passed by, I started realizing how much I liked her. I realized I loved her. But it was too late. I got everything that I wanted. Then why did I have to challenge my destiny and end up landing nowhere? Now when I was alone I thought I should not have taken admission in engineering. I would not have met her then. I really wish I had not liked her. Now I would not have missed her.

I was missing my friends too. I had stopped talking to them because of Riya. It hurt me more. Sameer was there with me always. We decided to go to Lonavala. I was ready to bunk college. We decided to go in the morning and come back by late evening. I took 2 packets of cigarettes with me. I was continuously smoking all the way to Lonavala.

'What is wrong with you? This is your eighth cigarette and we haven't reached Lonavela yet. Still 30 minutes to go,' Sameer shouted at me.

'Let it be. Now no one can stop me. I can live my life as I want. I am fed up with these tears. I will not cry for her anymore. From now on this cigarette is my girlfriend and I trust her. She can never leave me,' I said smoking another cigarette.

Sameer started driving the bike again. We reached Lonavala.

Sitting near the dam, we opened our first can of beer. I was thinking about Riya. I was wondering whether she really loved me. If she had, why did she leave me? And today if she left me, why was I still thinking of her even a 100 kilometres away? A few things are always left unsaid.

'Sameer, tell me something about my relationship?' I asked him.

'I didn't get you. What you want to know?'

'Do you really think Riya loved me? Or do you think I love her? What exactly is happening?'

I opened the second can of beer and gulped it down.

'Of course Riya loved you. There's no doubt about that. She loved you more than you love her. You never understood her. I know what she did is wrong but it had to end like this. She will understand some day.'

'I really want to curse Riya. She betrayed me. I want her life to be…' Before I could go any further, Sameer stopped me.

'You don't know what I am facing. I want to tell the whole world what we did. I will make her life…' Sameer shook me up.

'Stop it Aadi. Why are you cursing her? What will you get from it? I know you love her even today. Then why are you saying all these things?'

I closed my eyes and slept for sometime. We returned home by 8 pm. After that day, I started smoking regularly and soon turned into a chain smoker and a heavy drinker. I had started drinking regularly. Almost daily. I had stopped attending lectures as well.

One day, Sameer had some work in college. We went to the college together. Everyone who knew me was looking at me strangely. I could not understand the reason behind it. We went near the office. I saw Riya there coming with Amit. Amit was holding her hand. She was limping, as if she had hurt her leg. As she came near, I could see she was holding her stomach. Amit was supporting her. I left the office and went to the quadrangle.

'Hey where were you, Aditya? I hope you know Riya had an operation,' a guy from my class told me.

'What operation? What for?' I asked.

'She had an abortion.' I wanted to ask him who had told him that but he was gone. I looked at Sameer. He was as puzzled as I was. How? When? Why? Is it true? If then from whom? Amit or me? How could it be me?

Amit? Is she still with him? How can Riya do this? I don't believe it. Riya could never do this. She is smart enough to take care of herself. I wanted answers to all these questions.

I called her. She had changed her number. I called Amit. Even he had changed his number. I took her number from Swapnil and called her. I told her to meet me after an hour. She agreed and we decided to meet in the college.

She still could not walk properly. She looked upset.

'What happened to you? Is what I have heard true? You had an operation?' I asked her.

'Yes. I had an operation three days ago. I had messaged you on Orkut. Didn't you check it? I missed you when I was about to enter the operation theatre. I wanted you to be there.' She had tears in her eyes.

What was happening? I could not understand anything. She had admitted that she had an operation. I could not believe my ears. I was in tears. How could Riya do this? But she said she missed me. Did she mean that it was my child? She killed my child? But how could it be?

'Why did you have an operation?' My heartbeats increased.

'Operation for appendicitis. It's still aching,' she said.

Oh my God! I was relieved. She did not have an abortion. I would have died if it had been true. I calmed down. I was really happy and I left after saying bye to her. I still don't know why she missed me when she was with Amit now. But I didn't care. I wanted to stop the rumours which were spreading in college. Riya was clean. I knew it. However, I feared for her reputation. I trusted her but not Amit. I told everyone whom I could that the abortion rumours were untrue. I even hit a few classmates who challenged my explanation. They shut up after that. I knew my Riya couldn't do anything silly. But I also knew Riya was not mine anymore.

I went to a wine shop and bought two beer cans. Sameer joined me. He did not drink much but he gave me company. Even I didn't know why I was in a mood to drink. Was it because Riya did not have an abortion or was it because Riya was not mine?

'I am happy Sameer. Riya did not have an abortion. I would have died if it was true. Or maybe I still love her. Cheers.'

'If she comes to know that you are drinking so much and smoking too, how will she feel? She won't accept you in her life ever again,' Sameer said.

'She won't accept me anyways. Forget it. Let's just enjoy ourselves.'

Mom asked me about Riya several times but I ignored her. I did not want to spoil her image in front my parents. I still loved her. Mom tried calling Riya but she had changed her number. She somewhat got the hint that we had broken up. But she never said anything about it.

Shattered Dreams

My lifestyle, my likes, and dislikes—everything had changed, and so had my behaviour along. I had almost stopped attending college. Cigarettes and beer were the only things that gave me company. I had started cursing Riya. Whether it was done in a conscious state or not, I didn't care. I cursed her, her family, and her life.

The final defaulter list of the fourth semester came out. I searched my name on the list. My overall attendance was 52 percent. My attendance in ECAD 2 which Shinde sir taught was much less—45 percent.

I went along with all the other defaulter students to the head of the department. We were almost 25 students in total. But 5 students were in the limelight along with me. The rest were let off and only the five of us were asked to wait.

'I think you all are not interested in doing engineering anymore. It's okay. Now do one thing. Bring your parents during your submissions. In their absence, you will not be allowed to do them,' the HOD warned us.

He had asked us to bring our parents on purpose. He wanted us to feel embarrassed in front of them. I knew that if I told them about it, I would be killed. I thought of arranging 'paid' parents from somewhere who would act as my parents for money. This was the first time I was attempting to do something like this. I asked one of my classmates about it. He said he knew someone who could pretend to be my dad without taking any money. This was the last option I had. I thought of convincing the HOD one last time.

'I am sorry sir. I promise I won't repeat it. I will attend lectures regularly next year onwards. I had not been keeping well for a few days, that is the reason why my attendance was so low. Please forgive me sir,' I said trying my best to convince him.

'I don't want to hear a word from your mouth. You just need excuses for not attending lectures. I won't entertain your submission until you bring your parents. Now please leave and don't enter my office till you bring your parents along.'

'Sir, my parents are extremely busy. Can I make you talk with them over the phone? Please sir,' I requested one more time.

'No. Don't talk crap with me. All parents have time for thier children. Unless you bring them, you won't be allowed to do submissions this year. Take leave for a year and then come back,' he screamed at me.

I was left with no other option. I decided to bring

the paid person as my dad. But I knew it involved a lot of risk. If the staff realized what I was upto, I could be detained and not allowed to sit for exams. I decided to take the risk.

I met the uncle who had agreed to pose as my dad for money. I explained everything to him about my dad's work and about me. I also asked Sameer to come as my elder brother. No one in the staff knew him as he had dropped a year and we had different teachers. Moreover, he was in the civil department. I explained the situation to him. He was ready to do it for my sake. After our preparations were over, we started for college. I was scared. Still I gathered courage and went to the HOD's cabin.

'Sir, this is my dad and my elder brother,' I said introducing them. She asked them to take a seat. My heart was pumping rapidly.

'Do you know why you have been called here?' the HOD asked my dad.

'Yes. Becasue he had low attendance. Actually, the thing is that he was medically unfit for a few days and couldn't come to college,' my 'dad' explained.

'I understand. But they had been warned earlier. This is the final defaulter list. He had been warned last month too.'

Both my so called dad and brother looked at me.

'Sir, he will study hard and won't repeat it again in the future. I know he should have attended the lectures. I am pursuing engineering too and know how tough it can be. I am in my final year at Vivekanand College of Engineering, IT department,' Sameer said.

Why did he have to say IT department? I was scared. What if they asked him something he didn't know?

'What project are you doing? What is your percentage?' The HOD asked brother Sameer.

'I am doing a project on mobile technology. GPRS. And my overall percentage is 58 percent.' Sameer said.

I tried to control my laughter somehow. Sameer getting 58 percent was possible, but at Vivekanand College and in a project on mobile technology? That was funny.

'Learn something from your brother. You need to learn a lot. I am forgiving you this time. I don't want you to repeat this mistake again. Write an undertaking and leave.'

I went to Shinde sir because of whom my submission was delayed. He was not ready to accept my submission.

'Go and do your submissions in other subjects. I won't take your submission this year. Get out,' he shouted.

I did not leave his cabin. I was standing there along with Sameer and 'dad'.

'Sir, I'm really sorry. Please forgive me. It won't happen again. Please sir.'

He took my file and wrote fail on it and threw it away. He warned me to get out of the cabin. We didn't want to make him more angry so we left.

'Aadi, don't worry. He won't fail you. He is just trying to scare you and teach you a lesson. Don't worry, let's leave. The HOD has given permission. Shinde sir can't do anything about it now,' said Sameer.

We left college. I tried to ignore whatever had happened. I stopped at a nearby tapri and smoked a cigarette and drank a bottle of beer.

'Even if he gives me a KT in one subject, who cares? Let him do what he wants,' I said.

'I know. But keep concentrating on your studies. Exams are a few weeks away and you have vivas and practicals this week,' Sameer said.

I paid my actor 'dad' for his performance. Sameer dropped him near his house. I went home and tried to study, but I was not interested in it at all.

My vivas did not go very well. They were just good enough to get me passing marks. The same was with my practicals. I had to give nine theory papers. I did not even know what was in the syllabus. I wanted to clear at least five subjects to avoid dropping a year.

I tried to study with a beer in one hand and books in the other. It helped me to concentrate and leave my past behind. I gave my exams and was sure of clearing all the subjects. Except for drinking and smoking, there was no other activity left in my life.

Results were declared after two weeks.

I went to college and checked the result of the third semester.

Electrical networks	45	passed
Maths 3	53	passed
ECAD 1	28	failed

I knew this had been done on purpose. I was expecting to pass in ECAD 1. But I somewhere knew Shinde sir would take revenge. I checked out the fourth semester results.

Maths 4	40	passed
CSE	28	failed
Microprocessor	25	failed
PCom	40	passed
ECAD 2	25	failed
DD2	44	passed

I had got 4 KTs! I breathed a sigh of relief as I didn't get a drop for a year.

I took a look at the viva, practicals, and teamwork marks.

I had passed, except in:

| ECAD 2 viva | 8 | failed |
| ECAD 2 pracs | 9 | failed |

ECAD 2 termwork   7   failed

Four KTs in theory and three internal KTs. Seven KTs in all!

I was shocked. I would have to drop a year. I had cleared 5 theory subjects. However, Shinde sir had done it on purpose. I could not say a word. It was all over.

My mind said, 'Experience the first drop in engineering. Congrats. I told you to attend lectures and not mess with Shinde sir. Now enjoy yourself.'

What can be worse than this? First, you land up doing engineering and then you get your love. Later you lose your love and now lose a year. Everyone was going away. I needed someone who could take care of me. I would be screwed if I took this result home. I went near the IT section. Their result had been displayed two days ago. I looked for Riya's result. She had 3 KTs. But the important thing was that she had made it to the third year. Neha had passed too. All clear again.

I told Sameer about the result. He shouted at me saying he had told me to study.

I wanted Swapnil and Anup to be near me. I had broken my friendship with them just to avoid Riya. Today I needed them by my side, but they were not there. I had lost my best friends. Why? For Riya?

It's been almost six months since I had last spoken to the boys. We used to do everything together...laugh, cry, enjoy. It was hard to admit the fact that they were gone and I was afraid to talk to them again. Maybe my ego stopped me.

I wished to see them right now. I wanted to apologize to them and have them back in my life. They had already moved on with their lives, they had passed with good marks, and had made it to the third year. If Riya had been with me today, she would have told me to be strong and not to worry. But she was not there.

How could one walk away from someone they loved? It had been more than 7 months now but still her memories were fresh in my mind.

I wanted to take a different path now. I wanted to start all over again. I didn't want to forget her memories. I still remembered the time we had loved each other and the time when she left me. My life was at a standstill. She never once looked back even though I was still waiting for her.

My heart said she would come back, but I knew I should trust my mind.

Now, the cigarette was my only friend and girlfriend. I could kiss her anytime I wanted. I could feel her anytime I wanted. I could sleep without calling her and she wouldn't complain. Ashtrays were full during the nights. And the glass remained full during the days.

'Sameer, I am not going to tell my result at home right now. They will kill me.' I said to Sameer one day. I was sipping a beer.

'I think you should tell your parents about the result, Aadi. The date of the declaration of the result is printed on the mark sheet. They will get hurt if you hide it from them and they find out on their own later,' Sameer said.

'I can't tell them so early. In fact, I tried telling the result at home. But I was not able to. Even mom asked me twice. I ignored her question saying the results were late. I don't have courage to face them,' I replied.

All our dreams and expectations were buried in the sand. I had a dream of getting placed in a good company and earning lots of money. Now that dream couldn't be realized. I wanted my parents to be happy. That dream had vanished too. No son wants his parents to cry in front of him just because of a girl. But I could not forget her. She was more than a girlfriend for me. I was guilty of deceiving my parents. I had a dream of scoring good marks in the second year and convincing my mom that Riya was the best for me. But now that dream was shattered.

Wasted Hopes

I still can't understand how anyone can forget true love. I was trying hard to forget her. But couldn't.

Today I think if I had not liked you, I would not have loved you. If I would not have loved you, I would not have missed you. But I did, I do, and I will. It kills me to see that you don't care enough to stop me from walking away. It's not that I am mad for you, it's just that when I talk to you, I realize how much I love you and when I realize how much I love you, I realize I can't have you and that makes me love you even more. I am not supposed to love you, I am not supposed to care, and I am not supposed to live my life wishing you were there. I am not supposed to wonder where you are or what you are doing, but I cannot help it, because I am in love with you. There is this place in me where your fingertips still rest, your kisses still linger, and your whispers echo softly. It is the place where a part of you will forever be a part of me.

I could not cry all my life. I had to find a way to move on. I wanted to prove to everyone that I wasn't a loser. I couldn't fool myself and spoil my life. I wanted to achieve something. I wanted to prove to myself that I still had the confidence that I used to have earlier. It was not easy for me. It involved a lot of hard work.

It was September 9. It had been almost a year since I last saw Riya. I had never tried to contact her. She too hadn't. But there had been a few changes in my life. I had bought myself a bike from my own savings. It was a Hero Honda Karizma. I was proud of myself for having done something productive. When I was taking the delivery of the bike, I was missing Riya a lot. I wanted to tell her about my first big purchase in life. I wanted her to be the first person to sit on my bike. I wanted her beside me on this special occasion. My happiness would have doubled if Riya would have been with me. I sat on my bike along with my dad and went for the first ride. He was happy for obvious reasons. He had tears in his eyes. Even mom's eyes were wet. I felt proud at that moment. But somewhere I knew I was hiding the worst possible thing from them. Very soon I would have to tell them that I had dropped out. My dad hugged me.

It was an emotional moment for me. I would have been in seventh heaven if Riya too had been beside me. For the first time in the last few months, I was missing her very much. Until then I had thought Riya was a closed chapter in my life. However, everything flashed in front of my eyes today. I still loved her as much as I did before. I still remembered each and every moment with her. I wanted her back in my life. I couldn't live like this. Now that I had money, my parents were proud of me, I wanted her back. Attending lectures too was not a problem as I had a dropped out. I went to Aerol on my bike with Sameer. I waited near her building for two hours. But I could not see her.

'Let it be Aadi, let's leave,' Sameer said.

'I wanted to show her the bike. I was really missing her a lot. I could not forget her. I wanted her back. I wanted to give a last chance to our relationship. I hoped it worked.' We left.

I decided to bring her back into my life.

We came back to our place, chilled out for a bit, and then went to a bar. I was getting increasingly frustrated. The same thoughts were reverberating in my mind. Try as much as I could, my mind kept on going back to Riya. I ordered two bottles of beer.

'What has happened to you suddenly? Why are you drinking so much? I thought you had recovered and were moving on in your life,' said Sameer.

'I don't know, Sameer. Today when I got the bike keys, I was really missing her a lot. Even I had thought it was all over, but who am I kidding here? I can't forget her,' I said sipping the beer.

'She is not going to come back to you. She must be happy with Amit. Why you are spoiling your life again? Exams are so near. Why do you want her now? She is history,' Sameer reminded me.

'Please Sameer. I can't erase her from my mind. Even this alcohol can't. Let me give one last chance to my relationship. If I fail, then I will never think about her again. Please Sameer. Just one chance. Let me try to bring her back to me,' I was almost two beers down.

I ordered one more can of beer. Sameer tried to stop me from drinking. But I did not listen to him.

'Aadi, do you know what is happening in her life? Is she with Amit or not?' Sameer asked.

'I don't know what's happening and I don't care. I am going to give it a try. I will call her tomorrow. It is her birthday in some days,' I said.

We left the pub. I was heavily drunk and could not even walk properly.

'Why did you drink so much? Don't you have any responsibility towards your family, friends, and Riya?' Sameer asked with concern.

'Forget it. No one can stop me. I am not hurting anyone.'

'Why are you so stubborn? Don't you understand you are heading towards a dead end?' Sameer said.

Things were turning sour between us as he raised his voice and said, 'If you just want to do what even you know is bloody insane, then I am leaving.'

'Ok sorry,' I replied. 'I understand it's not the right thing to do, but I just don't want to face the real world. Not anymore.'

He gave me some water and we continued arguing.

If I think about it practically, I was really taking my life to a dead end.

No, I don't care, I don't love her. No, I don't want her back. I am happy, I am enjoying my life. Who says my heart is broken? Am I falling for her? No. I will sleep with other girls. And why should I think of just one girl when she just does not care?

Nevertheless, the fact was that I was just fooling myself by saying all this, as I still loved her, cared for her, and knew I would do it forever. So why did I let her go?

Why does someone love one person so much even after that person has betrayed him? I did not have any answer.

Thoughts

It's been more than a year since our break-up. Even today when I look back, I can still remember every small detail of the times we were together. I never knew our love was so strong. I went to meet her exactly a year after her birthday, but she was not ready to talk to me. She ignored all my gifts and my letters. I was so excited to meet her. I thought she would at least talk to me for a bit. I didn't expect anything more. But that too did not happen.

Even this year she was not ready to take any gifts from me. I don't know today if Amit and Riya are together. She did change her number after we broke up. Each day passed by thinking of her. I knew I had to concentrate on studies. But I could not.

Nothing would ever be right without her in my life again. Why the hell did she change her number again?

Whoever said that it was better to have loved and lost than never to have loved at all had obviously never felt this kind of love and the pain and destruction of life that the loss leaves behind. I could never see her anymore, and I knew that. I had a last chance on her birthday but it was gone.

On December 31 when I met Mr Banerjee, all the memories came flooding back. I thought about all that he had said after going back home. Each picture was crystal clear in front of me. Love can never be wrong, but a girl sure can. I thought about what he had said and felt he was right. I had made the mistake of loving her. I needed to move on.

I don't say I am still in as deep pain as I was last year when I tried to bring her back into my life.

Those were the worst days of my life. Though time has healed the wounds a little, it could never take away the desire to want her, to care for her, to cherish and love her.

She is and will always be my first love. There is still a part of my heart that wonders whether she really loved me in the first place.

I needed to move on with my life. Maybe Mr Banarjee was right. Love can never be wrong, but a girl can. I needed to accept the fact that she was not in my life anymore and move on. After all, life doesn't stop for anyone.

I needed to forget all the best moments of my life. I had to realize that Riya was not coming back to me again. She was happy with her life. She didn't need me anymore.

I forgave her for loving him. I forgave her for kissing him. I forgave her for sleeping with him. I forgave her for lying. All this did not hurt me anymore. What hurt me more was that she allowed him to touch her. She chose to go away from me. I have realized time can't be brought back. Was it my decision which forced her to go or her heart, it does not matter today. Today, I realize that true love hurts. I realize why people opt for one night stands or temporary relationships.

I gathered courage and strength and decided to forget everything. It was difficult, almost impossible. But I decided to do it. One thing that I would always think of is why did I let her go.

Exams were over. When the results came out, I came to know that I had cleared 1 KT. CSE. I still had one attempt in May to clear the other subjects and become eligible to move to third year. I decided to study hard this time and clear all my KTs. I wanted to move on. I called up Sameer.

'Sameer, I want to move on. I want to forget everything. I have thought about it well enough now. And this is my final decision,' I said.

'That's nice. I am glad to hear this. I was tired of explaining the same things again ans again to you. Thank God you realized it. I must thank Mr Banarjee,' Sameer said.

'I think God sent him on the earth for me. He knew everything about me. He was certainly no mere mortal and there was something special about him,' I said.

'Oh shut up! He was a normal human being. You were drunk. He was drunk. So stop thinking foolishly.'

'I want to tell you one more thing. I hope you believe it.'

'What is it now? Don't tell me you are in love again,' he said giving me a strange look.

'No, it's nothing like that. I have decided to quit drinking. I won't drink from now on. And I am serious. I will smoke but only once in a while, not like a chain smoker.' Sameer began laughing so loudly, he could not control his tears. I looked at him, trying to convince him that I was serious.

'Let us see how many days you can keep up with this promise. I will be happy if you quit.' He somehow controlled himself and stopped laughing.

But I had made up my mind.

Strange Incidents

I was in my bedroom, thinking of ways of telling my parents that I had dropped a year. In their minds, their son would be in the sixth semester now. But this wasn't the case. I did not have the guts to face them anymore. I was thinking about every possible solution. I looked at my cellphone. One message received.

It was an unknown number.

Good evening sir. I hope you have received a mail regarding your request. Thanks for contacting us.

I thought they had contacted me by mistake.

I replied, Hey, I think you have messaged on the wrong number. What are you talking about?

I got an instant reply, Is it Mr Suresh? This is Harsha here. You had contacted me in the morning regarding a job.

I replied again.

You are mistaken. This is Aditya here. I did not contact you. I don't have a job. I am doing

engineering at the moment and working on odd
part-time jobs.

I receive one more message.

Oh, I am so sorry. I think I messaged on a
wrong number. Thanks a lot. I am working for
a call centre in Malad. Sorry again.

I thought I could take help from her. One of my school
friends wanted a job. Maybe she was the appropriate
person whom I could consult about that. I thought of
continuing the conversation.

It's okay. My name is Aditya. I am doing
engineering from Euro college. Electronics
engineering. My part-time jobs help me earn a
decent amount for my myself.

She replied: Cool. It's nice to hear you're doing
something besides engineering. I too have been
working in this call centre for the last 6
months. Day shifts.

I replied: Nice to talk to you. If I have any work
I will call you or message you. Save my number.
Take care. Have a nice day.

I called her later. She did not attend it. I thought I was
disturbing her. I waited for her to respond. I got a reply
from her a day later.

Sorry. I was busy with my parents. Why don't
you give me a call tommorow night? Same time.
Take care. Bye.

I called her the day after. My mom and dad were sleeping. I was in my bedroom. She picked up the call. We greeted each other normally. She was speaking in a low voice. I could not hear her well enough.

'Why are u speaking so softly?' I asked.

'My parents don't allow me to talk at night. That's why,' she said.

'So why do you still want to talk to me? That's really strange.'

'Shut up. So which year are you in?' she asked.

'It's a long story. Actually I had to drop a year after second year at engineering and I did not tell my parents about it. They still think I am in the third year and I don't have the guts to tell them the real story,' I said.

'That's really bad. Do you realize that you are hurting them? Don't do this. They trust you so much and you are misleading them. Tell them the truth. I will help you if you want.'

'How can you help me?' I asked.

She suggested I message my parents if I did not have the courage to speak to them face to face or over the phone. She also told me that she would write an emotional message and send it to me on my phone. All I would have to do is forward it to my parents.

I told her that it was really considerate of her. Fifteen minutes later, I got a long text message from her that I had to send to my parents.

Sorry mom. Sorry dad. I don't know how you will react aftr reading this message. But your son has fooled you. Yes mom, I am fooling you. I am fooling myself. I am sorry for having given you so much pain. I wanted to tell you this since a long time but for various reasons, I couldn't. Mom, dad, I'm not in the third year in college, I'm still in the second. I had to drop a year. Please don't be angry with me. I did not have the guts to tell you. I tried but couldn't. Sorry mom. Sorry dad. I care for you both. I know my act is one big mistake but trust me, I really love you!! And I am here to change! So please let go of my mistake. I don't know how to tell you how truly sorry I am. I always blow your trust. But just once, please forgive me. I will study hard and clear all my subjects. Trust me. Give me just one chance to prove myself. I will do whatever you say.

That afternoon, I went out with Sameer. I decided to send this message at that time. I did not say anything about Harsha to Sameer. He would have killed me. We watched a movie and I messaged my mom after the movie.

Mom started calling me continuously after that. I did not pick up the call. I was afraid that she would be angry. I had committed a big blunder. I was ashamed of myself. I had fooled my parents for almost seven months. No son could have done what I did. I started crying. Sameer was consoling me. I received a message from mom.

Come home. Don't worry. We are always with you. Love you.

I started howling. I thought they would hit me or shout at me if nothing else. But they didn't say a word. This made me feel even more guilty. They had tried so hard to make me strong but I had never listened to them.

They gave me whatever I wanted. I still broke all the rules and their trust. The more they tried to bring out the best in me, the more I tried to ignore them.

'You have the best parents in the whole world, Aadi. They didn't even shout at you. Let's go home. I will come with you. Don't worry now and wipe away your tears. Listen to whatever they say. Don't argue with them even if Riya is discussed,' Sameer said to me while we were on our way back home.

We reached home. Mom and dad were sitting on the couch. It looked like they had had a big discussion. I went in and sat next to my dad. Sameer looked at me. He seemed scared. This made me even more nervous. I was waiting for them to start the conversation. But they didn't, so I finally spoke up.

'I'm sorry and I mean it. I won't do this again, I promise.'

'How many KTs have you got? Is there any problem with the college? Be frank with us. We want to know the truth today,' said dad.

'Dad, I tried my level best to clear the subjects, atleast the minimum subjects which would make me eligible for promotion to the third year. But I got an internal KT. Viva and termwork. So I was not eligible. I tried telling you both so many times but didn't have the courage to face you. I am sorry,' I replied with tears in my eyes.

'It's okay. But what have you decided to do now? Do you want to continue with engineering or not? Or do you want to change your stream? Are you capable of completing it?' dad asked me.

'Of course he is capable. He had scored good marks in HSC and also in the first semester. The main reason why he failed is something else,' mom shouted.

I did not say anything. I was at fault. I kept quiet. Riya was not the reason for my dropping a year. Beer was the main reason. It had made me complacent. I could not tell my mom about this. So I chose to keep quiet.

'Yes dad, I will. Give me one more chance. I will do it, I promise,' I said going closer to dad.

'It's okay. See to it that you complete your degree. We won't force you to work after that, but you should have a degree in your hands at least,' dad said.

I went to my room and messaged Harsha that everything was fine. She replied saying she was happy to hear that.

I kept thinking about all that she had done for me. Was I ready to take a chance with someone else? Could I take the risk of falling in love again? She had one of

Riya's qualities for sure—that of helping others in times of need.

But I had not even seen her till now. Everything was once again moving too fast. I told myself I needed to stop my heart from falling for her before it was too late. But I was also enjoying my time with her and wanted to see if things were going anywhere between us. This time was it lust or love with her? Whatever it was, it made me feel fresh and rejuvenated. I felt alive once again. This time with Harsha. A girl from a call centre. She must be a good looking girl. Call centres in Malad have extremely pretty girls.

I was falling in love once again. A girl whom I had never seen before and neither heard her voice clearly before but who was still doing so much for me. Initially I felt like she was a lot like Riya. But then I realized I should not be comparing her with anyone since she is her own person. I thought about giving myself another chance. Would Harsha be my second love?

Or was I attracted to her just because she had a few qualities similar to Riya? Caring, understanding, helpful.

God knows. But I wanted to move on.

I called her at night and I told her that I was attracted to her. She still spoke in low voice which wasn't very clear.

'Don't tell me. You're such a flirt. You should concentrate on your studies instead. And you must have a girlfriend for sure,' she said teasingly.

'No, I recently broke up and don't have a girlfriend now. How and why we broke up is a long story. She betrayed me even though I really loved her. Talking about studies, I don't care a damn about that. I just want to get to third year. I am also earning part-time. So who cares,' I said trying to ignore Riya's topic.

I did not have the guts to ask her where she lived. She might think I was getting involved with her. Still I tried to sound innocent and give her the impression that I was like the boy next door.

'What happened to your girlfriend?' she asked.

'She went off with someone else. Actually it's not her fault. I tried to stop her from going with him. He was not the right guy for her. I really cared for her.'

'What do you mean by the "right kind of guy"? What made you think so?' she asked again.

'He was my friend. I mean, I met him through her. But then we became friends and he had hatched a masterplan in his mind to get her. He fooled my little bachcha into falling in love with him. But it's over now. There's nothing for you to worry about,' I said trying to flirt with her.

'You still love her?' Her questions were never ending.

'It does not matter whether I love her or not. What matters is that she does not love me anymore,' I answered smartly.

'Who told you this?' she went again.

'Why are you asking me all these questions? Do you

know her? Or did we know each other before these calls? I felt something fishy.

'Nothing dear. I was just asking out of curiosity. If you don't like me asking, I won't. Is that fine?'

This was going too fast. My second would-be relationship and it was moving as fast as a speeding train.

'Can we meet tomorrow? I am free. I can drop by your office. I have purchased a new bike. What say?' I wanted to see her. I wanted to confirm that she was someone I didn't know before.

'I will tell you tomorrow morning. Is that fine?'

I agreed to wait. I received a message in the morning asking me to pick her up from the Eastern express highway. I got ready and went on my new bike. I was keen to meet her. I was in a good mood as I left my house that day, looking forward to seeing her for the first time. As I cruised down the road with the wind blowing through my hair, I thought to myself, Will she be like my Riya? Or will she be even better than her? I started imagining what she would be like from her voice.

But no one could replace Riya.

I reached the place. My eyes searched for a pretty face but I didn't see any. I could have waited there for a lifetime if it was for Riya. But it was Harsha.

I called her. She did not pick up. I messaged her. She did not reply to my message. I kept waiting for her for over an hour. I received a message.

I was just testing you to see if you were really going to come or not. Thanks for coming dear. I know you want to see me. I have mailed you my pictures. You can take a look. Bye. I will call you tonight.

This made me angry. I did not shout at her though. I did not want to spoil her day by fighting with her. I controlled myself. I used to get angry and spoil Riya's day. I didn't want to repeat the mistake. I replied to her:

It's okay dear. If you want me to drop you to your office, I will. No bad intentions. I never understood this when I was with Riya. Particularly around the last phase of our relationship. I don't want to hurt anyone now. Take care. Have a nice day.

I went home and opened my inbox. I saw her pictures. She was pretty, but not as pretty as my Riya. Brown eyes, fair, chubby cheeks, slightly overweight, and slightly on the shorter side. In all, a decent girl. I decided to flush out Riya from my life and give Harsha a chance.

It was the end of Riya and the beginning of Harsha.

Finally I could get rid of Riya's memories from my mind.

I messaged her: You look nice dear. Not perfect, but suitable for me.

She replied, Then who is perfect for you?

I replied: I am sorry if what I say hurts you. But Riya will always be the perfect one for me. No one can replace her in my life. But you have everything that a boy needs. Talk to you at night. Bye.

Unspoken Truth

I made up my mind to propose to her. If there was any girl who could help me forget my past, it was Harsha. I decided to propose to her the next night itself. I was waiting for the day to pass and the night to come. Maybe she was the girl I had been waiting for even since Riya left. She was the girl who could bring my life back. Bring my happiness back. I got tired of waiting for Riya. She couldn't hear my cries. She couldn't feel my tears. Only God knows what I was going through. All alone in the darkness. It was time to move on. Even though something in my mind told me to wait, I didn't want to anymore. I was tired of waiting and decided that this time I would propose to Harsha. Who said love happens just once? It could happen twice.

I went to my room and thought how silly I was to have not considered dating someone earlier. I should have taken this step long back. Riya wouldn't be back. Maybe our love story was not meant to be successful. God had some different plans in his mind. And I had to make my peace with that. I was going to give my life a second chance.

I called Harsha around 11 pm.

Harsha: 'Hi. Thanks for coming that day. Did you like my photos?'

Me: 'I want to tell you something.'

Harsha: 'Don't tell me you are in love with me.'

Me: 'Just close your eyes first.'

Harsha: 'What is it? Now you are scaring me.'

Me: 'I really don't deserve a girl like you. I am a flirt, I have the worst image, but I still want to change. I want to improve. I want a girl who can improve me. And that girl is you. I know Riya will always be somewhere in my mind. But I love you baby. And today when I saw your photos, I just wanted to hug you and never let you go. You are special to me. You make me complete. I will never leave you alone in this relationship. Love you. Do you wish to be my beloved?'

There was a long silence. I asked her to say something.

Harsha: 'Is this the first time you have said something like this to a girl or have you used these lines on other girls as well?

How could she know that I had proposed to Riya the same way? Or was she just guessing? .

Me: 'It's just for you. I have never said this to anyone before. And now I have a special song for you too. *Tujhe dekh dekh sona, tujhe dekh kar hai jagna…*

Again there was silence.

Harsha: This is surely not just for me. You have sung this for someone else too, haven't you? Tell me, am I right?

I became more and more suspicious. I was getting the feeling she knew me. How could she know all this? I had seen her photos and I couldn't remember seeing her before. Were her photos fake?

Me: 'I love you. I love you jaan. I love you my sweet little cute bachchu. Missing you.'

She didn't say a word. Nor did I. She was crying. My suspicions were confirmed after this.

Me: 'You are my bachcha. You are my jaan. You are my wife. Oh my god! I can't believe it. Tell me the truth. Please jaan, tell me. Please. You are my Riya, isn't it? You're the one who sent me fake photos.'

Still there was silence. It brought tears to my eyes. I could not believe what was happening. Was I watching a dream? When I was in a relationship, I let her go. I tried to forget her, but it did not happen. I tried to give a second chance to my relationship but she was not ready. I decided to get over her and got Harsha. I decided to propose to her. But I was again back to square one.

Me: 'Please answer me. Please.'

I started crying badly. I wanted to hear her real name. She was still sobbing.

Me: 'Please tell me. I know you are my Riya. It's time for us to grow up now. I know how much we miss each other. Please come back to me. You still have a place in my heart. I have been very lonely ever since you said goodbye. Remember those days when we both sang songs together, the smiles we shared each time we saw each other. Do you really want to throw away all those sweet memories? This is the only opportunity we have to rewrite our history. Just put away your pride and come back to me.

Come back. Please come back and rewrite our history.

She still didn't speak a word. This silence from her end was killing me.

Me: 'I know that we haven't talked for a long time, but that doesn't mean that I don't think about you everyday. You don't know just how much I wish that I could be lying there with you whispering in your ear my heart's deepest desires.'

I close my eyes and let my thoughts flow. 'I picture us lying in bed, your arms around me, my head upon your chest, my fingers gently touching your skin. My soft lips place a whisper of a kiss on your neck. I can hear your heartbeats getting louder and faster. In my mind, your lips capture me and hold me there in ecstasy. We look lost into each other's eyes. I feel your hands caress me as you whisper sweet nothings into my ear. You make sweet, sweet love to me and wipe away my tears. Each time that you touch me, it feels like the first time. As each night passes, your presence seems more real with me. But then I open my eyes and realize it was just another dream. Tears fall from my eyes. Pain sears through my chest. My heart cries out for you.'

And finally she spoke…

'I want to give you a love bite which will be visible to everyone. So that no girl will come close to you ever again. Let the world know that you are mine. Just mine. And that no one can take you away from me. I love you. Love you a lot. You are my kid. My bachcha. So innocent. So sweet. My Mr Perfect. I have tried so hard to fight these feelings, but I can't do it anymore. I know that I love you, but I didn't want to tell you. We had known each other only for a couple of weeks and you already had me completely and totally to yourself. I don't even want to think about being with anyone else. I thought that if I stopped talking to you, I would forget how I felt. I thought that if I could keep myself busy, I would be okay, but I can't forget you and I'm not okay. I am so overwhelmed by my feelings for you. I need to hear your voice. I need to feel your touch. I can't let you go. I feel terrible for not talking to you for the last few months. So many nights I have cried my eyes out in your absence. I broke up with Amit long back. He was not right for me. You were right. You are my Mr Perfect.'

Me: 'I have waited so long to be able to wake up every day to look at your beautiful face. I'm so thankful to God that you're here. You take my breath away with some of the things you say. I love the way I feel when I lie down with you, your arms wrapped around me holding me, like I'm your baby. I am sometimes surprised of how much emotion flows out when I cry over you. You say I'm perfect and that you're the luckiest girl in the world, but you don't see what I see when I look at you. I am so lucky to even have you touch me with your hands. Or to even look at me. I don't know what I did to deserve you in my life, but I thank God for letting me do it. You are so unbelievably perfect.'

We didn't realize how time flew. It was 7 in morning and we were still talking to each other. We decided to meet near the central garden at 2 pm.

When I got up, the world seemed beautiful. Everyone around me seemed to be happy. Suddenly my outlook towards people had changed. It was a positive start for me. The day which I had been waiting for had arrived. I was going to meet Riya, my love, after such a long time. I had forgotten her touch. I had forgotten her smile.

Did she still look same? I hadn't seen her for the past few months. I was thinking about her all the time. I wanted to feel her touch again. I wanted to see her smile again. I could not wait for the clock to strike 2 pm.

She had said once that I would never get a girl who could love me as much as she did. She was right. Now I was beginning to understand that love couldn't happen twice. It could happen just once. I was getting attracted to Harsha because she was not Harsha. She was my Riya. The days I spent without her, the nights I thought about her while looking at the stars, the dreams which involved her, the places where we went, the moments that we shared—everything was fresh in my mind. She told me that she loved me more than the world and that she couldn't imagine being with anyone else. We had such an amazing time when we were together. When I found out the truth about her, I was distraught, heartbroken, and felt used, foolish, and disgusted. I loved her more than anything in the world.

The moment I saw her, my heart skipped a beat again. The naughty smile was back on her face. She seemed tired. Maybe it was due to her hectic schedule. But I must admit she was looking more beautiful than before. More perfect than before. She had straightened her hair. She looked amazing. She came close to me and gave me a kiss. I looked around to see if anyone was watching us. She smiled.

'You have not changed at all. Why do you have to look here and there?' she smiled and kissed me again.

'As if you have changed. You are still the same. As always, you don't care a damn about the people around,' I said and caught her hand.

To be able to touch her after so long was beautiful. Riya was back. We decided to go to Grant Lane. She sat on my bike for the first time since I had purchased it. She put her arm round my waist and leaned against me. I kissed her. I asked her what exactly happened and how had she managed to get my new number. I asked her what went wrong with Amit? I had so many questions in my mind. We reached Grant Lane and sat on our favourite bench and she bagan telling me about all that had happened in her life in the past one year.

Revelations

'It was the beginning of a new relationship for me. It was not easy to forget the moments that I had with you. It was not easy to forget the places where we had gone. I never forgot you. Never did your thoughts leave my mind. The farther I went, the closer I was getting to you. I tried to be loyal to Amit. He was behaving very sweetly with me. He used to care a lot for me. I had requested him to give me some time to forget you and he agreed. I used to cry a lot when I was with him. When we went to Grant Lane, I cried for almost an hour. Whenever his bike passed central garden, I could not stop my tears. He knew everything. He was always with me. When I had an operation, he supported me a lot. I thought I had to give him the same love in return and kept telling myself I should not be thinking about you. I said sorry to him and told him this would never happen again. We always used to fight when you were the topic of discussion.'

'One day Amit said, "You are not happy with me I know. I can't make letters for you, I can't sing a song for you. I am simple. I can't give you surprises."'

'I asked him, "Why do you compare yourself with Aadi? I really don't understand why you have to bring him between us everytime? Have I ever complained about these things? Please Amit, stop comparing yourself with him." The arguments continued. It was not easy to adjust with him. As days passed, he started showing his true colours. He started avoiding me. He started shouting at me. "Don't you understand, you idiot? I am busy. I can't meet you now. So stop bothering me. I will call you when I am free," Amit used to say. And I would reply back saying,' 'What the hell. Aadi never used to do this. He always used to talk to me. He never gave me such reasons except for the last few days. We have hardly been together for 2 months and you are behaving so rudely. Aadi was right.'

'We started fighting daily. He never understood me the way you used to. He would behave nicely with me only when he wanted to take me to bed with him. One day your mom called me and said, "Riya is everything fine? Whenever I talk to Aadi about you. he changes the topic. Any problem?" I did not tell her what had happened between us. I told her that we both had decided to concentrate on our studies first and then think of other things. She accepted the reason and wished me luck for my future. She never called me after that. Maybe she understood that we both needed time to decide what we wanted.'

'Each day it was getting more and more difficult for me to be with Amit and live without you. I tried to forget each and every thing between us but it never happened. Many times, instead of taking Amit's name, I used to call him Aadi. Whenever we used to fight, he never cared to call me. He only cared just to be physical with me. I finally decided to tell him that I couldn't adjust with him.'

'I told him, "Amit, I can't forget Aadi. I love him. I still love him a lot. I am not going back to him. I have to pay for whatever I did to him. Maybe he will never forgive me, but I can't stop loving him. You are a fake person. You never loved me. Aadi was right. You can never love anyone. I lost my friend Neha because of you and my love too. Bye forever. I won't call you again."'

'He lost his temper and said, "Are you mad? You left Aditya because of me. And now you are leaving me because of Aditya. Are you so desperate to have both guys with you on bed?" I was really hurt about his comments and asked him, "Are you drunk? How can you say such a thing? You are cheap. Aadi was perfect. He always told me that Neha had the cheapest boyfriend in town. He was right. Get lost. I don't need you."'

'But he was not going to keep cool about it and said, "Bloody bitch. Even I don't need you anymore. I have used you as much as I wanted to—even though you didn't allow me to go all the way—and now your expiry date is up. You would remember Aditya whenever I tried to touch you. Get lost. Fuck off," and kept the phone down.'

'I really missed you that day. I wanted to call you. But I controlled myself. I still remember your message which said forget me and forget my name. I could not call you after all that I did to you. I was guilty. I was all alone. I had no friends and no love.'

'But problems kept coming one after the other. My dad's business collapsed. We had to sell our car. We had to sell our flat where we used to live. We did not want to sell the other flat. We kept it as it is. But it would have been too hectic for me and my brother if we shifted there. We rented a flat in Aerol in the same building. Still God had to test me some more. Both the shops which my dad owned were shut down. Suddenly financial problems arose. I could not take admission in the third year. I had to look for a job. I had no option left than to drop a year. I got a job in a call centre in Malad. I had a day shift there. I was the only person earning in my family. There was so much pressure on me to provide for my family that I could not think of coming back to you again. I had so many responsibilities on me. My salary was 12,000 rupees. Each day without you killed me from the inside. My schedule became hectic.'

'One day I got a message from you. I sent you a rude reply. The reason was but obvious. I did not want to be in a relationship again. I was frustrated with my job. Moreover I felt really guilty coming back to you after what had happened. If you had behaved the same way as you did in the last few days of our relationship, it would have increased my problems. I did not see any change in you when I met you on my birthday. I was going to the office. I saw that you had realized my importance but I still was not sure if I should come back to you. I already was so disturbed and was going through the worst phase of my life to solve this problem, I decided to change my number. I knew if I changed my number, you would not be able to contact me. I got busy in my routine work.'

'I had a client—Mr Suresh. He needed some urgent information by the end of the day. I did his work and messaged him. But you got that message instead. I checked both the numbers. There was a difference of just one digit. His number ended with 9061 and your number ended with 9060. I did not know it was your number. Then when you replied you were Aditya from Euro college I started chatting with you and began to keep in touch with you. And you, as usual, started flirting with me. In my call centre, it was compulsory to change the name in the calling department. I had changed my name to Harsha. I started talking to you using the same name. As our conversations began, I realized you still loved me. That brought a smile to my face. I still didn't reveal my identity to you. I wanted to see how far you were willing to go with Harsha. But you told me that Riya will always be your life. I felt you had changed. And here I am with you.

'I am sorry I thought wrongly of you. I could not see your love at that time. I am sorry for all the pain I caused you. I am sorry for the last one year when I was away from you. Can we be together again?' she said. She had fear in her eyes.

I was overcome with emotion and told Riya, 'Yes jaan. I am always yours. I can't forget the pain that you caused me. I can't forget the days when I needed you the most but still I was alone. I can't forget the time when I fought with the world alone. But I don't think much about these things. When I close my eyes, all that I can see is your smiling face. All I can remember is all the sweet moments that we shared. This time I won't ignore you. I am sorry for whatever I did. I should have given you time.'

I slept on her lap. I felt like I could die happily then. I looked into her eyes and started crying. She kissed my tears and played with my hair and cheeks. We had pani puri and paav bhaaji. My day was complete. Oh no! not yet. One thing was missing.

'Jaan , there is no one at home. Mom and dad have gone to watch a movie. They will have their dinner and come back late. We can go to my house. What say?' I said.

She agreed to come. When we reached home, we went straight to my bedroom and I closed the door.

We kissed. We hugged. We made love. We were lying naked on the bed. To make up after a big fight and a big break up feels really good. She kissed me. I kissed her back. While kissing her back, I remembered what Amit had told me—the black spot on her back was too hot. I observed carefully. There was no black spot on her back. This brought a big smile on my face. It meant he never touched her back, he was just fooling me. I loved my Riya. I always knew my Riya would never be wrong.

As we lay in each others arms, she asked me, 'Did you miss this?'

'Yes a lot. I always told you you're perfect. Your body is a wonderland. Love you a lot.'

'I won't leave you ever now. I am all yours. I realized what life is without you…love you too.'

'Jaan, what is Mr Suresh's full name? We should thank him. If it had not been for him, we would not have met again. What a coincidence it was. I thought something like this was only possible in Bollywood films. I still could not believe it happened with us in real life,' I said.

'I don't remember his full name, but let me check my mobile. I have his details there,' she said scanning her phone. 'Got it. His name is Mr Suresh Banerjee, Sales Manager.'

'What? Are you sure? Check it once again.'

'Yes dear. His name is Mr Banerjee,' she confirmed.

I could not believe it! It was the same person I had met long ago and who had shown me the right path.

He had said, 'Love is never wrong but a girl can be.'

I wanted to tell him that both my love and my girl were right.

I wanted to tell him she loved me. I wanted to tell him she cared for me. But a few things should be left unsaid.

Some love stories can never be predicted...

Epilogue

We loved, we fought, we broke up, and now we were together again. Everyone around me was happy as I had got what I had prayed for. I had never thought such a coincidence would ever happen with me. We never met Mr Banerjee after that. He had come into our lives to bring us together. I still don't know whether Mr Banerjee really exists?

Even though we are together today, we still miss Swapnil and Anup. We did not have their numbers, nor did Sameer. As we both had dropped a year, we never went to college. She had her job in Malad and I was busy too. Sameer was still a good friend. He always stood by my side.

Today when I have Riya back in my life, I have decided to quit smoking. I had already stopped drinking a while ago. We don't know where Amit and Neha are. Amit had called Riya once. She did not take his call. Instead she sent him a message saying she was back in a relationship with Aditya. He never contacted us after that. Neha was out of the picture. The cold war that had started between Riya and Neha didn't end. I did not interfere in solving it because it hardly affected our lives.

Though semesters were fast approaching, we didn't care about studies. I did not want studies to come between us. I never talked about it in front of her. I used to go to pick her and drop her to office daily. We enjoyed rides on bike together. We had started loving each other much more than before. Mom was not aware of it yet. I waited for the right moment to tell her. When God had given me everything I had prayed for, I had rejected everything and chose a wrong path which proved destructive. I had only one aim in life—Riya. That she was going to come back into my life was something I had never expected. We both had realized our mistakes and decided to stay together forever.

Riya accepted me for she knew I was the one who could bring happiness in her life, I was the one who could love her the most, I was the one whom she could rely and trust on.

However, was Riya's promise of love fulfilled? Was Aditya's promise of love fulfilled?

Few things left unsaid…

Some love stories never end! Their love story has not ended yet…

Acknowledgements

Firstly, I'd like to thank my love without whom this book would not have been possible.

Many thanks to Pankaj Ghodekar—a dear friend who stood by me while I was writing this script. I still remember how we chatted for 12 straight hours in those days. This book equally belongs to you.

Above all, a big thank you to my family—dad Jayant Nagarkar, mom Manju Nagarkar, and sister Shweta Nagarkar. Thanks also to uncle Ajay Palimkar, aunt Anuradha Palimkar, and last but not the least, my grandparents—Sulbha and Divakar Palimkar.

I would also like to thank my dear friends—Rohan, Saurabh More, Suhas Sonawane, Mugdha Naik, Sunita Shirsat, Pratiksha, Tushar, Anupkumar Rathod, Swapnil Indulkar, Pratik Dahale, Nilesh Pawar, Viraj Bandodkar, Vihar Paymode, Nilesh Yadav, and Mitesh Raut. They have all tried to improve me in some way or the other and it's commendable that they are still trying. I apologize if I have missed a few names.

Acknowledgements

A warm thank you to all the editors and the publishing team at Random House India. Special thanks to Milee and Gurveen for treating me as a friend.

A Note on the Author

Sudeep Nagarkar is the author of two bestselling novels—*Few Things Left Unsaid* (2011) and *That's the Way We Met* (2012). His third novel *It Started With a Friend Request* will release in July 2013.

Sudeep's books are inspired from real life incidents. They have been translated into regional languages and continue to top the bestseller charts.

He has a degree in Electronics Engineering from Mumbai University and is currently pursuing management studies from Welingkar Institute of Management. He is also a motivational speaker and has given guest lectures in various institutes and organizations. He resides in Mumbai.

You can get in touch with Sudeep via:

Facebook: www.facebook.com/sudeep.nagarkar

Twitter: www.twitter.com/sudeep_nagarkar

Facebook fan page: www.facebook.com/sudeep-nagarkarfanpage

Email: sudeepnagarkar@gmail.com.